Madison took a sip of the cognac, and as she set her glass down she saw a flash. A light reflecting off a metallic object in the darkness below the terrace. Then the tiny red beam from an infrared scope crossed Tahril's forehead. She reacted instinctively, without thought, leaping at Ahmed Tahril, knocking him over in his chair.

At the same moment, the crack of a rifle filled the air, the glass door behind them shattered. Madison drew her 9mm and moved to the edge of the terrace wall.

Bullets sprayed the terrace wall and dug into the house. The killer in the darkness had switched the rifle to automatic. Madison ducked, using the wall as a shield, then rose and caught a quick glimpse of the light bouncing off the rifle. She fired . . .

THE
PROVIDENCE
FILE

AMANDA KYLE WILLIAMS

The Naiad Press, Inc.
1991

Printed in the United States of America on Acid-Free Paper
First Edition

Edited by Katherine V. Forrest
Cover design by Pat Tong and Bonnie Liss
    (Phoenix Graphics)
Typeset by Sandi Stancil

Library of Congress Cataloging-in-Publication Data

Williams, Amanda Kyle, 1957–
    The Providence File / by Amanda Kyle Williams.
        p.   cm.
    ISBN 0-941483-92-4
    I. Title.
PS3573.I447425P7   1991
813'.54--dc20   90-22727
                                                      CIP

For Julie,
for everything.

ACKNOWLEDGMENTS

I send my warm thanks to the patient and generous people who contributed so much in so many ways to this book.

Dr. Mahmoud Albatel who most graciously took the time to speak with me about the beauty of his home country, Lebanon, and gave me his impressions of the Arab-Israeli conflict. His input was a vital part of the research that went into this book, and I hope I have done him no injustice.

My new friend, whom I shall call "Gerry," gave me some insight into what a woman in the secret world of Intelligence must endure, helped me guide Madison McGuire through her ups and downs, and promised to forgive me for the liberties I take here.

Steve Fischer, my very patient communications expert, for technical advice.

Tricia Watson, a loving friend whose wisdom and support I could not have done without.

Janice Brannon, who spent hours reading aloud and literally acted out parts for me so I could get just a bit closer to my characters.

Jeannie Michalosky, for cliche control.

My parents, Fred Kyle and Betty Williams, who contributed an IBM to the cause.

Margie N., for the loan that kept me writing.

Katherine Forrest, a fine writer, a wonderful and sensitive editor.

Barbara Grier, who has never been more than a phone call away, who makes herself available to her writers when they need advice or scolding or even when they need to be babied a little.

To my friend and partner Julie who bore the brunt of my frustrations and has been a rock in some of the most unsteady of times.

And finally, all the diligent writers and researchers before me who, by publishing their findings, have made my work so much easier.

PROLOGUE

Dry logs crackled in a huge stone fireplace, warming the room, sealing it from the chill of an Irish winter. Ahmed Tahril had spent much of his time over the last ten years in this safe house overlooking the sea near the Wicklow Mountains of Ireland. It was a good country. It provided him with an escape, a safe haven, and deniability, while his army of liberators, as he liked to call them, carried out his orders around the world.

Tahril sat in a heavy leather chair, his arms on the armrests, his feet flat on the floor. He stared absently through the picture window at the rocks below, smooth and water-beaten. If he was satisfied by his recent accomplishments or preparing for a victory it was not evident on his face.

He stood, plunging his hands deep in his pockets, moving closer to the window. "They call us terrorists," he mumbled to himself, barely above a whisper. "They have not yet known true terror."

Tahril turned to see Karl Speigel enter the room, his square jaw thrust out, a tight smile on his wide face. Speigel was not a tall man but he was powerful, with the look of a weightlifter, his forearms short and wide, shoulders rounded, biceps straining his shirtsleeves. "The eyes of the world will be on the plight of the Palestinian, Ahmed. You're doing a great thing for your people, for your country."

Tahril's brown eyes hardened at that. "The Palestinian people have no country."

* * * * *

He sat in first class accommodations, his body rigid, muscles tensed, black eyes fixed on the seat before him, oblivious to the chatter of the passengers around him who spoke excitedly of going home for Christmas. He had not relaxed since leaving Frankfurt, nor had he accepted food or drink. He would allow himself no comforts, never wanting to forget his purpose.

Forty-five minutes out of London, where the Boeing 747 had picked up the last of its two hundred and sixty-nine passengers, the young man turned cold eyes to the tiny window on his left and peered out intently. Beneath the cloud cover he saw what he had been looking for: the deep blue waters of the North Atlantic.

Welcoming his destiny, the young man calmly pressed the code key on his lap-top computer, pushed the device under his seat and slowly walked to the center of the aircraft, where he dropped to his knees and screamed his battle cry in broken English: "Death to the Great Satan!"

A sudden and eerie hush fell over the Pan American flight as all eyes turned in horror to the young man. If anyone fully understood the meaning of the terrible words shouted by the stranger at thirty thousand feet, no one reacted, no one made a move. And those words, those horrible threatening words seemed to be momentarily suspended in time, hanging over the aircraft, echoing the fate of each passenger.

Seconds later the airplane burst into thousands of pieces, littering the North Atlantic with its doomed cargo.

There was no time for pain. No time for homecomings or reconciliations. No time for goodbyes.

* * * * *

The passengers for El Al flight 1030 sat in the waiting area at the Athens airport only moments away from boarding their plane for Tel Aviv.

An Israeli woman scolded her two children and ordered them to sit down. A young couple, apparently musicians, their violin cases at their side, held hands and watched the planes taxi up and down the runway. A middle-aged man read a magazine and chain-smoked, much to the distress of his wife who occasionally waved a hand in an attempt to clear the air around her. Two American teenagers laughed as they tried to make sense of an Athens newspaper. Others sat idly, some impatiently, as people do in airports, waiting for their boarding call.

At length a side door opened and an airline employee stepped through to announce in several languages that boarding would now be permitted. All but two passengers began to form a line. The two that remained, it was later reported, were the young couple who released the latches on their violin cases and withdrew their instruments: Uzi submachine guns.

The couple opened fire on the El Al passengers. Twenty-six were immediately killed, including the Israeli woman, her two children, and the two American teenagers. The couple continued firing until they escaped the airport and climbed into a waiting automobile.

Over eighteen-hundred rounds were expended, and a total of thirty-four people eventually died from the murderous assault. Another eighty were seriously wounded. And none of the injured or dead could have known that they had been carefully chosen targets in a war where the number of civilian casualties and innocent victims was simply a part of victory.

CHAPTER ONE

The cool rays of December's sun pushed their way through grey clouds, occasionally reaching the rolling tide and illuminating a splash of spectacular white. Winter waves crashed against the rugged Carolina beach as Madison McGuire, dressed in a heavy cable-knit sweater and jeans tucked into hiking boots, began her afternoon walk, avoiding only by inches the cold water that rushed in to attack her feet.

Several yards behind her trotted a straggly white cat which had apparently decided to adopt her. The little beggar had appeared on the deck of the beach house a few weeks prior, exhausted, thin and wounded. Terry, Madison remembered, had urgently transported her to the local vet, for Terry Woodall was incapable of seeing any living thing suffer without taking immediate action. Four days later the animal, which they now affectionately referred to as Stray Cat, was returned to their beach home and had since assumed permanent residency. Madison smiled as Stray Cat toyed with a sand crab, one dirty white paw slapping playfully at her prey.

Madison walked several more yards before hearing the muffled sound over the roar of the water. She looked up, shielding her eyes. She was not prepared for what she saw. It was down on the beach before she could move, its giant shadow covering her, its blades whipping the wind in her face.

She strained to see who was stepping out of the government helicopter and walking deliberately towards her. First she saw the slight build, then the narrow face, the dark glasses, and finally the outstretched hand.

"Madison McGuire?" the man asked, extending identification. "Greg Abbott, State Department."

Madison, letting the outstretched hand go unattended, answered coolly, "What can I do for you, Mr. Abbott?"

Greg Abbott gathered the collar of his overcoat closer around his neck. "I have some business to discuss with you. Can we walk?"

Madison looked at the man for several seconds before answering. "I agreed to semi-annual debriefings to assure you people that I'm not a security risk. I didn't agree to walks with State Department officials. I'm officially on the shelf, Mr. Abbott. Retired. Any business you may have does not, thankfully, concern me. I'm not cleared anymore."

Abbott smiled. "You've been cleared for this. It's a field assignment. Interested?"

A storm was coming, the wind picking up. The roar of the ocean mingled with the ringing in Madison's ears. "Team or single?" she heard herself asking. The words had left her mouth involuntarily, the natural, irrepressible curiosity that had been nurtured and promoted during her training — as it was in the training of all spies.

"It's a single assignment. Infiltration."

"Target?" she inquired, feeling a rush of adrenaline.

Satisfied that he had her interest, Abbott smiled again. "You'll have to give us more of a commitment before I give you that information. I'll tell you this much. I've read your file. I know what you went through on your last assignment. And believe me, we wouldn't re-activate you unless someone up there thinks you're the right person for the job." He walked back to the helicopter.

Brushing the sand off his shoes, he looked back at Madison. "The new Director would like to see you tomorrow. Eleven o'clock at Langley."

Madison watched the chopper lift up off the beach, the sand under it swirling chaotically, watched the dark clouds gathering in the sky. There *was* a storm coming, but it had little to do with rain or snow or wind. It was a storm called *The Company*, and once again it had caught her off guard, blasted her at full force before she could prepare.

She folded her arms across her chest and shivered as she walked back towards the beach house.

* * * * *

It was ten forty-five a.m. in Langley, Virginia, when Madison stepped out of the blue BMW in the visitors parking lot and took a deep breath, studying the seven-story white stone structure in front of her.

How odd it had seemed when the guard at the gate directed her to the visitors section. However, the feeling of being merely a visitor was forgotten as soon as she pushed open the doors and stepped inside the headquarters of the Central Intelligence Agency.

The white tiled floors, the numerous security guards with their jackets open, to give easy access to weapons, the color-coded badge she was given to wear, all seemed perfectly natural. The sound of heels clicking down long, sterile halls, the clean almost antiseptic smell seemed to soothe her somehow and flooded her with memories. Memories of eighteen years of service to her country.

Why now did those memories suddenly seem so comfortable? A year ago all she had wanted to do was get out alive and never come back. She smiled a bit sadly as she waited to be escorted to the seventh floor, remembering something that she had once read: "Pain has an element of blank; It cannot recollect." How poignant those simple words seemed now.

"Madison," a voice exclaimed from behind her. "Good to see you again." She turned and saw Fred Nolan, his round face beaming, his hair considerably thinner than when she had last seen him. "I heard you were coming in today and I wanted to greet you personally. It's been a long time." He took her hand and shook it enthusiastically.

Madison smiled. "How have you been, old man?" She remembered that Fred Nolan worked with top secret video tape that came into Langley, specializing in analyzing statements and reactions of agents, new recruits and informants who were not aware they were on camera.

They stepped in the elevator and the stainless steel doors closed with a metallic thud. "You're looking at the new Deputy Director of Intelligence," Nolan stated with a rare flush of pride.

"Well, congratulations, that's quite an honor. No one deserves it more than you."

The elevator doors opened on the seventh floor. Nolan said, "Take a right and give your name at the checkpoint down the hall. Someone will show you to the Director's office. When you're done, call me and we'll get some lunch."

Madison touched Nolan's sleeve gently. "Tell me about this new Director. What's he like?"

"He's a mean old bastard. It's a job requirement," he said with a smile and left her there in the empty hallway.

As she walked the bare corridors of CIA headquarters Madison searched her memory for what she knew about Mitchell Colby, the new Director of Central Intelligence.

In 1959, after many years as a field operative,

Mitchell Colby was appointed Station Chief to the Havana office and worked under diplomatic cover there in perhaps the most difficult and dangerous times in CIA history. Later he became an observer-advisor on the Intelligence Advisory Committee, and it was no great surprise when the new administration appointed Colby to the position of Director of Central Intelligence, the largest Intelligence gathering agency in the world, and the principal Intelligence advisor to the National Security Council and the President. Now Colby's CIA was enjoying more freedom under this administration than it had since the fifties, the disgraces of the seventies all but forgotten.

She gave her name to one of the guards at the final checkpoint and was escorted another twenty yards to the Director's door.

A deep, raspy voice answered her knock and instructed her to enter. "Hello, Madison," the grey haired gentleman said, rising from his desk and crossing the room to greet her.

"Mr. Colby, your reputation precedes you, sir. It's an honor to meet you," she replied sincerely.

The Director seemed surprised. "Good God, you're British, and beautiful too."

"With all due respect, sir, I am very much an American. I merely speak with a bit of an accent," she snapped. She cringed at the harshness in her own voice. But she had struggled with her looks all her life. It seemed she either drew too much attention to herself or too little respect. She had become proficient at the techniques of disguise because she had discovered early on in her career that in order to be effective in the field one must be able to blend into a crowd, go unnoticed.

Mitchell Colby seemed unaffected by her tone. In fact it seemed to please him greatly. He tilted back his head and let out a great and overpowering laugh, his fleshy cheeks jiggling. "You'll have to pardon my ignorance. I should have realized you'd have an accent. I know you were very young when your father was transferred to England. Please, have a seat, Madison," he invited, walking to the other side of his massive desk and sitting down in a high-backed chair. It was the type of chair one would expect to find in an executive office — with the exception of the tiny holes punched in the armrest where the Director had repeatedly, and probably unconsciously, stabbed the point of his pen.

"I knew your father, by the way," he told Madison. "Jake McGuire was one of a kind. A true hero." And then with a softness in his voice that Madison hadn't expected, "You must miss him very much."

"It's been over twenty years since he was killed," she answered, hoping the conversation would soon take a new direction. She had never been particularly comfortable with familiarity from strangers, no matter how sincere it seemed.

Mitchell Colby turned to a small table behind his desk and poured two cups of black coffee from what looked like the very first drip coffee maker made. He passed one cup across the desk to Madison, then took a sip of the other and shuddered slightly. "I've been going over your file," he said, fingering the edges of a manila folder lying on his desk. "I hope

11

you won't be embarrassed when I say that you were one of the most effective operatives we've ever employed in the field."

"That's very kind of you, sir," Madison answered without embarrassment.

"You know, they say the day of the single operative is over," he continued thoughtfully. "What with all the artificial intelligence we have available to us now. But I'm from the old school. In my opinion no satellite, no technology can replace good old human intelligence. It takes a unique person to do what comes so naturally to you and me. That feel for the field. That ability to read people, to anticipate their next move, their every reaction. Those instincts can't be replaced by any gadget, no matter how sophisticated it may be." He looked up from the folder, his clear grey eyes resting idly on her. "I have monthly reports from the head of your transition team, Marge Price. The first couple of months were pretty tough, huh?"

Madison became more uncomfortable. Yes, she had had her bad days, but she wasn't at all sure she wanted to confide in this man. "It took a while to adjust," she admitted reluctantly. "I was a bit uneasy with my retirement in the beginning."

"That is precisely the point I wanted to make. You always will be uneasy, as you say, with your retirement. You're like me in that way. We've devoted our lives to this business. We know it. It's something we understand. You're a fish out of water, Madison. How long can you live the way you're living now? How long before those quiet afternoon walks on the beach and dinner at six sharp begin to strangle you?"

Madison sat back hard in her chair. Had they been watching her? Or had Marge Price's reports simply included the fact that she walked on the beach in the afternoons? In the beginning those walks had been something vital to her existence. They had served as a lifeline of sorts. When she left the National Operations Intelligence Service, the CIA's most clandestine unit, those walks had been a symbol of her new freedom. A symbol of a new life. A life without pressure. A life without bloodshed, without betrayal. A life insulated from the influence of a government that had nearly destroyed her.

The Director, seeing that he could not draw her out, went on. "Would you like to know what conclusions Marge Price has made about your transition from agent to private citizen?"

"Mr. Colby, Marge has become a very close friend. I'd like to keep it that way. Perhaps it would be better if I didn't know."

Colby chuckled. "Marge has nothing but praise for you. She feels that with time you will make a place for yourself in what she calls the real world . . . I see here that you've been offered a teaching position at a Boston area university. Why haven't you responded to that offer, Madison? It's been three months now. . . My theory is that you're afraid to commit to anything outside *this* Company. You want to do something you know you'll excel in, and there are no guarantees in that world out there."

There was some merit to what he said, Madison admitted to herself. "Are you offering me a job? Or just a one time assignment?"

Colby smiled a nice grandfatherly smile. "A job, Madison, if you want it. Why we ever let you go in the first place is a mystery to me."

"But then, the CIA never really lets anyone go. Do they, Mr. Colby?"

Mitchell Colby was at first surprised by the bitterness of her reply, by the fact that there was not a hint of emotion on her face. But then he looked at her, suddenly aware that there was so much of the other in each of them. Like himself she had been trained to withhold herself calmly and steadily without revealing intent or emotion. And he knew that which may be a great asset in the dark world of undercover operations was, in fact, a social inadequacy of sorts, an obstruction in the area of personal relationships. Wasn't it his wife who had always complained that he was incapable of expressing his deepest feelings? He both respected and pitied these qualities in Madison, knowing full well that, like him, she was what she was, partially due to the fact that the Company had molded her and trained her to suppress that natural need one has to relate one's fears and hopes to those close to them.

He stood and walked her to the door. "Think about it, Madison. We'll be in touch."

* * * * *

It was a long drive back to the North Carolina beach house from Langley. Still, Madison was glad for the time alone. She needed it to consider Mitchell Colby's proposal, and she needed time to figure out how to approach Terry, who believed

14

Madison had gone to Langley for a regular security check.

Terry was stretched out on the couch, a book lying face down on her chest, eyes closed, with heavy lashes resting on her flushed cheeks. Madison watched her silently for a few minutes. The sight of her lover always stirred something inside her. She never failed to be moved by the enormous, almost unsettling love she felt for Terry.

Terry opened her eyes slowly as if she had felt Madison's presence there, and sighed sweetly. "How was your trip?" she asked softly, holding out her arms.

"Interesting. How was your nap?" Madison asked as she sat down next to Terry on the couch.

Terry Woodall, who believed that afternoon naps were one of life's most precious luxuries, yawned and stretched. "Luscious," she answered, stroking Madison's cheek, and then, sensing that something was wrong, she asked, "What is it?"

Madison got up and pushed open the glass doors that led onto the deck. "They want me back," she said quietly, resting her hands on the railing, looking out on the water. She shivered as she spoke, only partly due to the cold wind coming off the ocean.

The fear formed slowly at first, as Terry allowed her thoughts to stray. Then it rose inside her, hitting her at gale force. How she had dreaded this day, knowing it was inevitable. She had seen Madison growing more and more restless, if not discontented. Now the CIA had come for her. Approached *her*. She spoke quietly, as if this new

15

reality had turned to ash in her throat. "What did you say?"

Madison turned to her. "I gave no answer. I wanted to think it over, talk it over with you."

Terry got up from the couch and paced back and forth. "You actually have to think it over? Have you forgotten what we went through? They almost killed you." She felt her heart pressing harder against her chest. "Oh, God, I knew this would happen. I knew they'd try to take you away from me again." She fell helplessly onto the couch.

Madison sat next to her. "Darling, no one is trying to take me away from you. No one could. I love you." She leaned forward and kissed Terry's forehead, and then the closed eyes, feeling the tears that had gathered on thick lashes. Terry drew her closer and Madison felt the need in her. The need for that particular kind of intimacy that dulls all insecurities. The need to reaffirm that Madison was still hers.

Madison stood and began slowly slipping out of her clothing, in invitation. And Terry answered the invitation without hesitation, running her hands along Madison's sides and over her bare hips, then resting her head against the smooth stomach, letting one hand glide between Madison's thighs.

She felt Madison shiver, felt Madison's breathing stop for a moment, felt Madison's hands holding he head, gently pulling Terry to her. She felt Madison slowly parting the thick red hair for her. And she wasn't quite sure why she felt so terribly sad at that moment, or why she could not stop the tears that rolled down her cheeks when she felt Madison come,

16

or why she did not want Madison's thin hands to stop touching her for even a moment.

* * * * *

Much later in the evening when they were on the couch, Madison leaning back into the soft cushions, and Terry resting her head in Madison's lap, Madison made the mistake of bringing up the subject of the Company. "You see, darling, you've done something constructive with your time," she explained quietly, feeling Terry pulling away from her. "You've finished school. You've passed the bar, you're starting your own practice. And what have I done? I've stayed in shape. I suppose that's something. I've read countless books, all of which have confirmed that I'm frightfully out of step and hopelessly incorrect politically. I've begun my memoirs, only to have the agency tell me I'd be prosecuted under the National Security Act if I attempt to publish them. And recently I've begun to believe I can communicate telepathically with Stray Cat. I need —"

"I thought this was what you needed," Terry broke in, not at all diverted by Madison's attempt at humor. "You wanted time for all those things you were denied for so long. Quiet time. Free time. Relaxation, reading, writing."

Madison lit a cigarette and walked to the window. "I *did* think it was what I wanted. I truly did. It's odd because in many ways my life is so complete now. We're in love, we're happy . . . I just feel an absence of direction. It's unsettling. Don't you see, darling? I'm not ready for retirement. I want to try another go at it. I don't know in what capacity. Analysis perhaps. It doesn't have to mean going back into the field."

"Oh come on, Madison. You think they want you back to sit you behind a desk? Or maybe you think they'll give you a title and a big office in honor of all your heroic acts. Maybe they'll make you Director one day." She paused, realizing that her words sounded harsher than she had intended. "I just want you to be realistic. You're a woman and you're a lesbian. How many of either have ever made it out of the field and into the front office? They keep people like you hidden. You'll never get any recognition. They'll use you and then they'll get rid of you. You're expendable."

Madison stubbed out her cigarette and turned to Terry. "This isn't about recognition. I don't want to be the bloody Director of Central Intelligence. I just want to work again."

Terry studied her silently for a moment. "You know, I'm just beginning to understand you. You thrive on conflict. You can't be happy being contented. You fought and ran for so long that you don't know how to live a normal life. Just when everything is working for you, you have to do something to screw it up."

"Thank you, Doctor, for that insightful observation." Madison snapped.

Terry waved a hand in frustration. "You've already made your decision, haven't you? I can feel your distance. Some deep dark little part of you has already entered the world of spookdom. Why did you even bother consulting me?"

"Because I thought you would understand," Madison answered, running a hand through her hair, trying to contain the sharpness in her voice.

"I understand that I'm losing you. I understand that you won't be satisfied until you get yourself killed in some senseless, secret war because you've bought into all the things they've told you about patriotism and national security and the fucking greater good."

"Terry, darling, I'm the very same person you fell in love with. I haven't changed one little bit. Those things were all characteristics you loved about me, that you found different and exciting. I'm still the same person."

Terry did not answer, and Madison turned back to the window, knowing that they would never agree.

* * * * *

A blinding sun reflected off the snow, making the concrete landing pad barely visible through the evergreens. The pilot patiently circled once and surveyed the area. The security on the ground, the pilot observed, was absolute. One guard was posted at each entrance to the house and three others watched the landing pad, radios in hand, semi-automatic pistols tucked securely in their jackets.

Not even the pilot, who had received top priority clearance, knew how many more eyes watched from quiet posts in the thick Virginia woods to assure the safety of the government strategists who sometimes gathered here for clandestine meetings.

Officially this place did not exist. Not in any

records. Not on any map. And, as always, the select few pilots allowed access to what was code named the Summer House had been instructed to log no flight plan. The sole purpose of this place was to provide a safe meeting ground for top officials in planning the nation's most secret Intelligence activities. Strategists and planners who could not meet in the nation's capital without the eyes of the media or some adversary agency upon them, particularly in these troubled times.

The government chopper hovered over the landing area, casting a great fluttering shadow on the snow before setting down with one final tremor. The pilot removed her dark glasses and offered a smile to her passenger. "This is as far as I go, Ms. Price. Someone will see you to the door."

The side of the chopper opened, flooding the interior with light, forcing Marge Price to shield her eyes. Slowly a set of metal steps came into focus, and a man dressed in civilian clothes standing next to them. "This way, please," he said pleasantly.

The sprawling white brick house tucked neatly in the woods was larger than Marge had remembered. The high gloss parquet entrance hall seemed to go on for miles. She stood just inside the front door taking in the low beamed ceilings, the polished oak doors, the occasional armchair covered with a deep, velvety emerald green.

"They're waiting for you in the library. Fourth door on the left," the escort announced politely.

Mitchell Colby greeted her informally. "Thank you for coming on such short notice, Marge. Would you care for some coffee before we get underway? I think you know everyone here."

Marge did indeed know everyone present. She had met all of them, worked with some, and seen many like them come and go over the years of political change. They wore different suits and different expressions but basically, whether on the right or left wing, they were the same mix of good and bad, selfish and selfless, ambitious and dedicated.

Marge said her hellos and joined James Jefferies, the Secretary of State, at the coffee pot, while Mitchell Colby positioned himself at the head of a long conference table and waited with tired eyes for everyone to be seated.

James Jefferies and Greg Allen Abbott, the head of the State Department's little known Intelligence Division, sat on Colby's right. William Ryan, the Deputy Director of Plans for the CIA, and Fred Nolan, the Deputy Director of Intelligence, sat on Colby's left. Marge Price took a seat at the other end of the table, facing the Director.

Mitchell Colby began speaking even as the chairs were being scooted forward by their occupants, his voice low, grave. "As you all know two hundred and fifty Americans and another nineteen people lost their lives when an American jetliner was blown out of the skies over the North Sea a few weeks ago. Yesterday two Americans and dozens of Israelis were gunned down in the Athens airport. We've been scrambling to collect enough Intelligence to piece this nightmare together, and now we think we've pinned down the terrorist group responsible. We're here today to make some decisions and hopefully agree on a solution. Between the CIA, the State Department and the other agencies involved, we should be able to do just that."

The Secretary of State began to speak, a troubled expression on his normally placid face. "On December seventh the State Department was made aware of a threat called in to one of our diplomatic facilities in Europe. The caller indicated that there would be a bombing attempt against a Pan Am flight flying from Frankfurt to the U.S. The origin of the call is still —"

William Ryan broke in, his anger obvious. "Jesus, are you saying the State Department knew about this and took no action?"

"What could we do, Bill?" asked Greg Abbott of the State Department. "We get dozens of calls like that every week. You know as we all do that if we can't verify the reliability of the source we can only take a couple of steps. We notify our embassies, and we notify the FAA which in turn notifies the airline."

"Who in the hell notified those two hundred and fifty Americans on board?" Ryan snapped.

"Mr. Ryan," the Secretary broke in, "you're fairly new at this, and although we appreciate your enthusiasm and certainly share your outrage, you must remember that we're here to plan an operation that will find the ones responsible for this massacre. We are not here to find fault with our own system."

The rebuke from the elder statesman seemed to subdue William Ryan. He sank back into his chair and sulkily sipped at a cup of coffee.

"Has anyone claimed responsibility?" Marge Price asked.

"Every crazy bastard and radical group in Europe has placed calls to our embassies trying to take the credit," answered Colby, his grey face twitching with tension, his jaw clenched tightly. "Tell them what we've got, Fred."

"Blowing up an airplane in today's world, even for an accomplished terrorist organization, is a difficult task," Fred Nolan began, looking into each face at the table as he spoke. "It takes big money, sophisticated technology, and the expertise of an accomplished bomb maker. Our Intelligence tells us that there is currently only one group organized enough and wealthy enough to pull off an operation of this magnitude. They call themselves The Providence Liberation Army of Palestine. Their training camps are located somewhere in the Bekaa Valley, and, as I told the Secretary yesterday, we're reasonably sure their headquarters are in Frankfurt, Germany."

James Jefferies added, "Based on that Intelligence, we've had some discussions with the West German government. However, it's a very delicate situation for any European government. They don't deny that the Providence headquarters are located in Frankfurt, but they won't confirm either. In their eyes any cooperation on their part with the U.S. or any retaliation would only invite terrorist attacks against their own citizens. Especially since this particular group is generally motivated by the Palestinian problem. No government wants to be seen as siding with the U.S. or Israel. Essentially what I'm saying is that we'll get no help diplomatically from Germany. And, as you know, the President has ruled out a military response. Without proof it would be diplomatic suicide."

Mitchell Colby turned to Marge Price. "We wanted you involved in this discussion, Marge, because as a behavioral expert we need your input. Obviously we're in quite a predicament."

Marge Price looked at the Director, puzzled. "I'm far from being an expert on terrorism, Mitchell. You know that. I'm way out of my league here."

"I understand that," Colby said patiently. "But I wanted you to understand our problem completely before we agreed on a solution. At this point our only real alternative is to attempt to infiltrate Providence. We'd like to send one of our operatives in there and we need your opinion as to her readiness."

"Which operative?" Marge asked.

"McGuire, code name Scorpion. What do you think?"

Marge Price, feeling the perspiration in her palm where she gripped an ink pen, swallowed hard. Madison was her friend. How could she give a strictly professional opinion without considering what the consequences might be for Madison? She knew that an okay from her could send Madison back out in the field. "Madison McGuire was de-activated a year ago," she answered feebly.

"We want to re-activate her. What do you think?" he asked again.

"Well, she's healthy, mentally and physically. She's got the experience."

"Yes or no, Marge," Colby insisted. "Is she ready for a field assignment?"

"Yes," Marge answered quietly.

* * * * *

Terry and Madison were just finishing dinner when the telephone rang. Madison answered. "It's time, Madison," Greg Abbott said. "There's a small airport outside Edenton, North Carolina. Be there in the morning at nine. I've made your travel arrangements. We'll have a nice long talk and you'll be back home by evening. Any problems?"

"No. I'll see you then." Madison replaced the receiver and turned to look at Terry, who was solemnly clearing the table. "They want to see me tomorrow. I'll have to leave early."

"Fine," Terry answered with less emotion than she felt and walked into the kitchen, knowing that the distance between them was growing. She leaned against the counter and looked out the kitchen window. Then she felt Madison's arms wrap around her, felt Madison's breath on her neck. But it wasn't enough. Because what she felt most was their world coming apart.

"Please don't do this, Terry. Don't shut me out completely," she heard Madison say, but she could not bring herself to answer. Instead she turned and walked upstairs, leaving Madison alone in the kitchen.

CHAPTER TWO

The landing was relatively smooth considering the condition of the remote landing strip, which looked as if it had been abandoned years ago. The pilot had been friendly and had chatted freely during the flight. He was married, had two children, loved baseball, and wished he could get home more often. Naturally no names had been exchanged, which was just good tradecraft, standard procedure — another nameless face in her career.

The hangar sat at the end of the landing strip, a run-down tin building with a rusted roof. It was bright inside, with rows of fluorescent lights overhead. One small card table sat near the door with two folding metal chairs. So much for the glamour of the spy business, she mused.

The door opened behind her and Greg Abbott walked in. Madison smiled. "Well, I must say, Mr. Abbott, when you said you'd make my travel arrangements I didn't anticipate a three-hour flight." Then, gesturing towards the small table and chairs, she added, "I see you've spared no expense."

Greg Abbott grinned and offered his hand. "No expense at all, in fact. I hope the flight wasn't too unpleasant for you."

Madison pulled out one of the chairs and sat down. "Not at all. I'm very curious, Mr. Abbott, as to why you felt all this security was necessary. Even I don't know where I am."

Abbott sat down and leaned back in one of the metal chairs, crossing an ankle over a knee. He looked directly into her eyes when he spoke, something that most men seemed to have difficulty doing. "If you accept this assignment we want to do everything possible to insure the success of the operation. That means keeping you away from D.C., any government installations and government officials. It's imperative that our target believe you've severed any ties with us. Once Operation White Flag gets underway, I'll be your sole contact. You'll be given information you can use, depending on where you are, in case you need to tip us or get out in a hurry."

He paused and leaned forward, elbows resting on the table, one hand holding his chin. "I'm telling you this now, Madison, so you'll know we'll be there for you this time. We're not going to turn you loose out there. That's a promise. What happened with the Club Twelve operation was tragic. I want to be sure you understand that your country didn't betray you. One man did."

"I assure you, I wouldn't be here if I believed anything else. Still, I'm curious as to why I've been chosen for a field assignment. I've been out of the field for a year. My contacts are probably stale. I'd be going out there cold. Surely you have other operatives who are better prepared."

"You were chosen because of your background. We don't even have to create a cover for you. It's already there and it's perfect. If anyone runs a background check, and they will, all they'll find is that you were one of our top operatives, you were sent out on an assignment, got set up and nearly killed. Obviously this could have made you a little bitter. Perhaps you might even want to strike back against a government that screwed you over. See what I'm getting at? Who would question your motives?" He leaned back in his chair again, eyes gleaming.

Madison saw that Greg Allen Abbott was a man who loved his work. "So, if and when I go back into the field, whoever you're running the operation against would be more inclined to trust me than someone they knew nothing about?"

"Exactly. And it doesn't hurt at all that rumors are still floating around the underground in Europe about the ruthless and dangerous female agent who called herself Scorpion and had the sting to back it up. True or false, those rumors can help us now."

Madison lit a cigarette. "But if anyone does run

a check they'll see I've showed up for my debriefings and passed my polygraph tests. I've been a very good girl."

Abbott pointed one thin finger at Madison. "You underestimate us. We'll alter those records. On the surface your file will show that we lost track of you shortly after your last assignment. Only those cleared for this operation will know the truth."

"Tell me about the target," Madison said, satisfied with Abbott's answer.

"A group that calls itself Providence. Ever hear of them?"

Madison winced. "That's quite an ambitious project, wouldn't you say? Besides being extremely radical, they're very powerful and well-funded. It's a bit naive to think any one operative could disband a group like that, don't you agree?"

"We don't want you to try and disband the group. We want you to join the group," Abbott answered flatly.

"I see," Madison responded, pushing her chair away from the table. "Well, Mr. Abbott, thank you for a very interesting day, but I'm afraid you have the wrong person."

Greg Abbott smiled. It was a good, practiced smile and Madison wondered vaguely if that smile had been part of his training.

"This isn't something we dreamed up yesterday, Madison. We've been planning this operation for quite some time. It was just a matter of finding the right person. We've already figured out how to get you in. All you have to do is go along for the ride, verify the location of their training camps, and let us know when the head of the group is at the camps. His name is Ahmed Tahril, and by the time we're finished with the disinformation campaign we have planned, he'll beg you to join up."

"What about your Intelligence? Can't you find Tahril and the camps on your own? You have satellite photos, reconnaissance aircraft —"

Abbott interrupted. "The problem is that they seem to know when to expect a satellite pass and during those hours they move all the equipment, people, weapons and automobiles inside the buildings. And since the Bekaa Valley is sprinkled with camps that have nearly identical buildings it's very difficult to be certain we have the Providence camps. Providence is state-sponsored and has access to Libyan, Iraqi, Syrian and probably even Soviet Intelligence. They track our satellites, they protect Tahril and provide him with travel documents and whatever else he needs. It makes it nearly impossible for us to put a finger on him. When we move on the Providence camps, Madison, we have to be a hundred percent sure we have the right camps because the Bekaa Valley is under Syrian control. That leaves no room for mistakes. Syrian troops could be in the camps within fifteen, twenty minutes."

"What happens to Ahmed Tahril when you hit the camps? What happens to the rest, the recruits?"

Abbott cleared his throat and shifted in his chair. "What happens to Tahril is not our problem. We're not cleared for the rest of the operation. Our problem is getting you in and out safely. I'm told we'll mobilize immediately after you're dispatched so we can be there to get you out within an hour of your signal."

"Why Providence? Why now? They've been operating for years."

Greg Abbott leaned forward and spoke quietly, his eyes locked on hers. "Because Providence planted the bomb that took two hundred and sixty-nine innocent lives on a flight to the United States over the holidays. Think about how many lives that bombing affected. Christmas will never be the same for the families of those people who died on that plane, Madison, never."

Madison looked up slowly. She had seen the newspaper reports of the bombing, seen the faces of parents and friends waiting in the airport when they had learned that the plane had been blown out of the sky. She had heard their screams, heard them weep, seen them collapse in disbelief. "I assume I'll be briefed," she said with the quiet determination that had made her a legend in the field.

"We'll take you to a special compound and give you a refresher course in explosives prep, improvised weapons, et cetera, et cetera. And, yes, you'll be briefed completely. By the time you get there you'll know what type of underwear Mr. Tahril prefers." Abbott stood. "We'd like to get started as soon as possible. We'll give you a few days to clear up any loose ends and then I'll arrange transportation. Are you with us?"

"Yes, Mr. Abbott, I'm with you," Madison answered and then stood there in the empty hangar long after Greg Abbott had left, wondering how Terry would react. Wondering if they would argue, wondering if Terry would be there when she came home from the field, and knowing it would not be fair to ask.

* * * * *

It was an unseasonably warm February day in Washington, D.C. The temperature had already reached sixty degrees and the streets were crowded at the lunch hour, as they always were. But somehow on this day the hurried pace of the nation's capital did not disturb Terry as it normally did. Perhaps because she was preoccupied. Perhaps because a clear and cloudless day could brighten up even the most solemn of cities.

Terry had had an appointment with a prospective client and, finding herself free by noon, had decided to ring Marge Price at her State Department office and make a date for lunch. Marge had been delighted. She cleared her schedule immediately and, knowing how difficult it would be for Terry to get a table anywhere in the city at that hour, called her favorite restaurant.

After giving Marge Price's name to the tuxedoed waiter, Terry was seated in a separate dining room with green plants hanging from the ceiling and tinted skylights that bathed the room in a warm, pale light. The conversation was low and muted, and Terry, feeling very much like an intruder and not wanting to look at the vaguely familiar faces of senators and congressmen at the tables around her, ordered Perrier and stared out the window at the Lincoln Memorial in the distance.

As she glimpsed Terry in the back room, Marge Price smiled, the normally stern face showing a softness about it that few ever saw, certainly not her male counterparts at State who secretly referred to her as "the barracuda." A heavy-set woman in a dark blue suit and flat shoes, she walked deliberately through the restaurant.

As Terry watched her approach she was struck, as she had been on many occasions, with the lightness in her step, with the confidence she seemed to radiate. Marge was well into her late fifties and her years in D.C. as a behavioral expert, who carried the burden of analyzing the readiness of operatives for clandestine operations, were taking their toll. Her once sandy brown hair was nearly all grey now, the lines around her eyes seemed to add a wisdom to her face.

Terry, standing to greet her, was met with a warm embrace.

"Your call was such a nice surprise. What on earth brings you to D.C.?" Marge asked.

"A new client, I hope. It's tough to build a practice though when you don't have much of a track record, and most of the big guns here already have good tax attorneys."

Without being asked, the waiter delivered a scotch and soda for Marge and more sparkling water for Terry, and the two women fell silent as he placed their drinks on the table.

Marge studied Terry knowingly. "We'll need a few minutes," she told the waiter. Then she asked, "This is about Madison, isn't it?"

Terry was thankful for the directness that came so natural to Marge Price. "I don't know what to do, Marge. They want her back. But you already know that. As the head of her transition team they must have consulted you. How could you have recommended her? You know she isn't ready."

"I didn't recommend her. I simply gave my

opinion as to her readiness." Marge glanced around and then leaned forward. She spoke quietly over the table, as if she and Terry were conspirators in some secret plot. "Listen, you and Madison are my dear friends. But I can't allow that friendship to cloud my professional judgment. Madison is quite capable of carrying out a field assignment, and from the reports I've seen she is apparently very receptive to the idea. God knows I wish she weren't. But it's her decision and I simply cannot interfere."

Terry sighed and leaned back in her chair. "It isn't fair, Marge. Madison didn't consider my feelings at all. Oh, she asked how I felt, but not until she'd already made her decision." She leaned forward and whispered, "Tell me about this assignment. Is it safe?"

"You know that's classified, Terry. Please don't ask."

She was losing control now. She felt herself flush, felt her anger growing. "Jesus, Marge, do you have any idea what it's like for an ordinary person to try to live in *spook-central?* Never getting a reasonable answer. Never knowing what the hell is going on. I don't know if I can go back to living that way."

Marge touched her hand gently. "I understand. You have some very personal decisions to make, Terry. But first I want you to try and understand the situation completely. Madison spent nearly half her life learning her trade. She's one of the very best, and she wouldn't take this assignment if she thought she couldn't pull it off."

"That's not the point and you know it."

"Yes, I know. You feel betrayed. You feel you've been left out of something that has a direct effect on your life. And in a way, you have been, just as every person who has ever become involved with an undercover operative has been left out. There are certain things that you may never be able to be a part of in Madison's life. It's the nature of the business. And you're right, it isn't fair to the ones who get left at home."

"When we started living together Madison promised she'd stay out of it. She wanted out, at least she said she did. She told me all she wanted was to be left alone, with me. She said she loved me more than anything else."

"Terry, you must understand that her need to work again does not reflect some sort of inadequacy on your part. This often happens with agents who go into early retirement. It's very difficult for them to feel as if they belong in our world." She paused. "Listen, if it's any help to you, I know the man personally who would be Madison's contact. He's young, and bright, and he's experienced at running agents in the field. He's good, Terry, very good. He'd pull her out the minute anything went wrong."

The waiter returned with fresh bread and the lunch orders were placed. Terry absently buttered a piece of bread and then set it aside, uninterested. She looked past Marge as she spoke.

"Barely a year ago, I sat in a cottage outside London with Madison. A bullet had grazed her neck and she'd been stabbed in her shoulder and chest. I sat in there wondering when the door would fly open and someone would bust in and kill her, kill us. It was the most frightening experience of my life." She turned her eyes to Marge and fought back the tears. "I can't do it again, Marge. As selfish as that may seem, I don't think I can handle it. I just want a normal life."

Marge frowned, and when she spoke there was sadness in her voice. "No one could fault you for that. I just don't know what to say. You want me to tell you it's okay. I can tell you this. I really do understand that you have to take care of yourself. Madison will understand that too. She wouldn't want you to be unhappy."

* * * * *

It was after eleven when Madison returned from her meeting with Greg Abbott. The lights in the house were out, and she noticed at once that Terry's Honda was not in the garage.

Stray Cat rubbed against her legs as she opened the door, then ran past her into the kitchen to voice her complaints over finding an empty food dish.

Madison stood in the dark living room for several moments. Old habits were hard to break. It had been part of her training so many years ago to always pause when you enter a dark room. Wait silently. Feel the room. Feel any other presence that might be lurking there. Listen with your mind . . . It had served her well over the years. At length she switched on the lights and went to the kitchen where she filled the kitty dish.

She saw the light blinking on the answering machine as she walked back to the living room. "I decided to stay the night in D.C." Terry's voice was distant, removed. "I don't want to say goodbye to you, Madison . . . I can't. I know you've made your decision, and I really do understand that it's what you need to do. I just can't live with it. I'm sorry. Please, make it easier on both of us and leave before I get home tomorrow afternoon."

The machine clicked off and Madison sat back hard on the couch. She wasn't sure how long she had been staring at some distant point on the wall, when the telephone rang.

"Are you all right?" Marge asked.

"Yes . . . You've seen Terry?"

"We had lunch today."

Madison was silent for several seconds. "She's leaving me."

"Madison, she's so young and she's frightened. She hasn't learned yet that she can't arrange life in a nice neat little package. Give her time. She'll come around."

Madison replaced the receiver slowly. She walked upstairs and pulled a suitcase from the closet. Half dazed, half numb, she began filling it, folding each item neatly.

Not a tear fell that night. Her pain, her aloneness became her strength, a self-imposed emptiness that her darker side seized and nurtured and protected with morbid resolution. She was untouchable now. It was what she wanted.

CHAPTER THREE

Greg Allen Abbott had just walked into his fashionable Washington, D.C. apartment, which sat high atop the Saratoga Building overlooking chic Connecticut Avenue. He loosened his tie and took off his Bally shoes, carefully placing them on a shelf in a closet on his way to the kitchen. He poured a wine glass of club soda. He had given up drinking any type of alcoholic beverage almost a year ago. Not that he had a drinking problem. It was simply an issue of control.

His telephone rang just as he sank back into the

deep cushions on his sofa. With a sigh he answered, "Abbott."

"It's Maloane," the female voice reported. "Thought you'd want to be kept up to date. I got some interesting dialogue from the tap. It seems your secret weapon has just been dumped."

Abbott propped his feet on the coffee table and smiled. "Good. That was a distraction she didn't need."

"You know then that she's a lesbian?" Katherine Maloane asked, unable to hide her surprise. "Does anyone else know?"

"No way. There were rumors a few years ago, but the former director buried them, never let it go into her file. And I'm going to make sure Mitchell Colby never finds out. The old bastard would probably scrap the whole operation because of some senseless homophobic policy that no one but Colby and his deputies give a shit about anymore. I could care less about her preferences as long as she performs in the field."

"Well now, I had no idea you were such a free thinker," Maloane said with a grin in her voice. "I'm impressed."

"This is to go no further. Understand?"

"Understood," Maloane said.

Greg Abbott replaced the receiver and took a satisfied sip of his club soda. Everything seemed to be falling into place so nicely.

Although he was a young man by Washington standards, his political ambitions were highly concentrated. Being the controller in an operation that could bring down The Providence Liberation Army of Palestine and destroy the most dangerous terrorist mastermind in the world was no small task. It would stand out on the resumé, add to a long line of successes. Successes that would eventually make him the Assistant Secretary of State. James Jefferies had already promised him that. And from there possibly the Senate, and then the highest executive office in the nation would be only a few short years away.

Of course there were a few details to take care of before he was in a position to run for any elected office. A wife was a must, but that shouldn't be difficult. There must be many women as ambitious as he. And although he could not offer a woman physical intimacy, he could offer wealth and position. That would be enough. There were a lot of marriages of convenience in Washington, D.C. He knew he would not be the only gay politician there. And he had accepted staying in the closet as a way of life. It was part of survival in Washington. And Greg Allen Abbott's survival instincts were strong indeed.

* * * * *

The approach was made at night, under the cover of darkness. The runway lights had been turned on by remote control and then extinguished as soon as the plane had landed safely.

Madison was not sure where she was. The flight from North Carolina had taken barely an hour and a half. Now, walking from the plane to a waiting van, she could smell the salty air and feel a warm breeze against her face. She was near water, she had traveled further south. But that was all she knew.

A woman climbed out of the van as Madison approached. She was tall, and as the door opened and the inside lights came on, Madison could see that she was blonde and thin with wide athletic shoulders.

The woman slid the side door of the van open and tossed Madison's suitcase in the back. "Welcome to your home for the next couple of weeks. I'm Katherine Maloane."

"Madison McGuire." They shook hands.

"I know who you are. You're the reason I've been assigned to this island paradise. Climb in."

The van began to move down a narrow road. In the path of the headlights Madison could see sandy soil and an occasional palm tree. "Where are we?"

"You got me," Katherine answered with a smile. "I came in last night and the pilot didn't want to share that information. The government is very secretive about its private islands, you know. It's probably supposed to be owned by some rich Republican."

Madison noticed her southern accent. She reached in her bag and pulled out one of her long brown cigarettes. "Mind if I smoke?"

Katherine shrugged. "It's your body. Of course you'd live longer if you didn't."

Madison ignored the comment. "Where are we going?"

"A house about a mile from here. It's incredible. I've been having a blast all day. I spent half the day lying on the beach. It's so beautiful here I hate to see Abbott and the others get here tomorrow."

"Why did you come in early?"

"They owed me a day off. Anyway, they won't be

here until tomorrow afternoon, so we can relax and enjoy."

"What I want is to get to work. I've had enough relaxation time."

Katherine turned and looked into Madison's bright green eyes for the first time. "God, you're uptight. Lighten up a little."

Madison sighed and took a long drag from the cigarette. Why did she have to be stuck on an island with a woman who seemed intent on offering unsolicited advice?

Katherine Maloane had been right about the house. It was incredible, a huge white stucco home on a hill overlooking the ocean, and surrounded by palm trees with an enormous rock garden in the center of the front lawn. The interior was no less impressive. High ceilings, a black and white marble-tiled entrance, chandeliers glistening over-head, a spiral staircase that opened into a lavish living room.

Katherine turned to her and smiled when they entered. "There's an olympic-size pool out back and eight, count them, eight bedrooms upstairs. Take your pick. I'm starved. Want some dinner?"

Madison had started up the stairs with her suitcase. "Sure, if it's no trouble. I'll just be a few minutes."

Ten minutes later she found her way to the kitchen. Katherine was on her way out with a tray of sliced French bread, cheese, summer sausage and olives. "Hope this is okay. I don't cook, so it'll have to do. Grab some wine, would you?"

Madison followed her into the living room. She put the tray on the coffee table and then sat on the floor. Katherine stretched her legs out under the glass-top table and leaned against the couch.

"What's your function here?" Madison asked after she had nearly finished her dinner and had two glasses of wine.

"To help you prepare for your assignment. I was assistant director at the Center for Strategic and International Studies at Georgetown University before I came to work for the government a couple of years ago. I specialize in counter-terrorism policies and objectives. I asked Greg to let me be a part of your preparation team."

"Why?"

Katherine took a sip of wine and dabbed her mouth with a napkin. "I've heard a lot about you. I wanted to see for myself if you're as good as they say you are."

Madison refilled her own glass and was surprised to find that they had finished the wine.

Katherine disappeared momentarily and returned with a fresh bottle. "Frankly," she said, sitting down on the floor next to Madison as if they had known each other all their lives, "you're not what I expected."

"And what exactly did you expect?" Madison asked, slightly amused.

"Someone bigger, tougher, and not so damn British. I've heard you're a real hard-ass."

Madison felt the wine for the first time, felt the warmth of it in her stomach, felt the lightness in her head. "You're very direct," she said with a smile.

Katherine propped an elbow on the couch and looked at her with an interest Madison could not define. "As long as we're being direct, tell me what it's like to sleep with someone of the same sex."

Madison swallowed her wine slowly. "You seem very sure that I can answer that question for you."

"You're a lesbian. It's only logical that you could," Katherine answered, nonchalantly popping an olive in her mouth, and washing it down with wine.

Madison smiled. "I see. I didn't realize it was so obvious."

"We've had a tap on your phone. That's how I found out." She paused and waited for Madison's reaction. When none was forthcoming she said, "I mean you've been away for a while, we had to check you out."

"Of course," Madison said evenly, thinking that she should have known.

"I hope I haven't offended you. I'm just curious," Katherine persisted.

Madison leaned back against the couch and studied her. She had known women like Katherine before, some merely curious, others struggling with their sexuality.

"I don't know what to tell you, Katherine," she said, half amused and a little uncomfortable. "It's not something I know how to explain."

"Oh, I think you do," Katherine said in all her directness, and moved closer to Madison.

Madison knew what was coming next, and Katherine did not surprise her. She leaned forward and kissed Madison. It was a soft, tender kiss. The kind of kiss that was sensual in its uncertainty. The kind of kiss that waited for an answer and pleaded for a response. And Madison did respond, although she wasn't entirely sure why she responded so

44

quickly, or why one gentle kiss from a stranger sent tiny, tingling waves through her stomach. Perhaps it was merely that she was feeling a bit drunk. Perhaps it was the power she felt. The power to reject or accept this woman's advances, without reservation, without commitment, without complication.

She touched Katherine's chin, bringing her mouth closer, pressing harder against her lips this time. Katherine's mouth was warm and wet and the bittersweet taste of red wine still lingered there. She felt Katherine's hands under her shirt and her nails in her back. "Show me," Madison heard her whisper as she ran her tongue along Madison's neck. Her breathing was irregular, her breasts pressed against Madison, wanting to be touched. Madison opened Katherine's shirt. Katherine slipped out of her shorts. Her body was thin, but strong and well-shaped. Her breasts were firm and round, the nipples dark brown, erect.

Madison brought a knee up between Katherine's legs and watched as Katherine moved sensually against that knee, cupping her hands around it, holding it tightly against her.

Tugging off her own clothes, Madison leaned over on top of her and kissed her lightly, pulling away after each kiss, teasing her until Katherine wrapped her arms around Madison and refused to let her pull away again.

Katherine's skin was salty and smelled of musk and sun, and at that very moment Madison McGuire forgot what was facing her or what was past.

* * * * *

The light of morning trickled into the bedroom. Madison opened her eyes slowly to a strange room, her head pounding. She showered, brushed her teeth and found a bathrobe hanging on the bathroom door.

Katherine was sitting at the kitchen table. "Well, good morning," she said cheerfully, kissing Madison softly. "Want coffee?"

"Please," Madison answered, and when Katherine set a cup in front of her, she began the speech she had rehearsed in the shower. "Katherine, last night was wonderful, but I have to be honest, I'm in love with someone else. I'm not prepared for another relationship right now. I —"

Katherine smiled brightly. "Relax. My life is complicated enough. Let's just have some fun and enjoy each other. No strings attached. Deal?"

"Deal."

"Good. Madison, you look like you feel awful. Want some tomato juice? Works great for a hangover." She smiled impishly. "I can't help you out with the guilt, though. You'll have to deal with that on your own."

CHAPTER FOUR

In the ancient land of Lebanon's Bekaa Valley, near Baalbek between the Lebanon and Anti-Lebanon Mountain Ranges, a farmer prepared his land for planting. The short and relatively mild winter had nearly passed. In the months to come the fertile land of the Bekaa would yield a magnificent crop of vegetables, barley and plump grapes.

Even sooner though, a new crop of terrorists would emerge from the Bekaa. Young recruits who were paid the equivalent of one thousand dollars a month while they learned their new trade in one of the nearby camps. They were mostly young, mostly poor, mostly male, and nearly all of them Palestinian Arabs, some of whom had never before been away from the filth and squalor of the refugee camps.

These young recruits were being trained in a variety of techniques, ranging from the simple, such as escape, evasion, and crowd incitement, to the more advanced, which included weapons handling, hostage taking and even manning surface-to-air missiles.

They were first evaluated by the camp's trainers. The extent of their training depended a great deal on their intelligence level. In many cases simply knowing how to attach a detonator or pull a safety pin on a grenade was all a potential terrorist needed know. It did not take a high degree of intelligence to open fire on an unsuspecting crowd at a sidewalk cafe or to toss a grenade in a car window.

The Providence training camps were among the most sophisticated in the Middle East. The funding, for the most part, came from Libya, Iraq and Syria. The weapons were supplied by the Soviets and included the most advanced hand-held weapons and explosives available. The pay-off for these countries was well worth the investment. With each attack, particularly if the attack was carried out against seemingly innocent bystanders, came disruption and destabilization.

At this hour in the camps the focus was media manipulation. The recruits were sitting on the floor in one of the twelve aluminum buildings, their full concentration on the speaker, Abu Khaled, a Palestinian.

Khaled was a master of manipulation. In June of 1985 he and eleven other Palestinians had hijacked a TWA flight from Athens to Rome. One of the thirty-nine American passengers on board was killed, but not until the world's media had been summoned. Before the horrified eyes of the world, a young navy sailor was murdered and dumped on the runway. The message was clear. No more lives would be taken if forty-two Arab terrorists were released from Israeli prisons. Ultimately these demands were met. Khaled and the others were given safe passage to Libya, where they celebrated yet another victory.

"Above all," Khaled was saying, his voice loud and strong, his eyes fevered and dark, "you must never forget your purpose. Regardless of your emotions, you must be patient, stay in control and wait. The media will come to you. We need publicity because it is generally followed by two reactions: sympathy or outrage. And when the world becomes sympathetic to the plight of the Palestinian people, my friends, the world's people pressure their governments to take action against our oppressors. And when the world is outraged, they pressure their governments to take some steps to resolve the conflict. Either way we win."

He smiled at the young recruits. "Tomorrow you will leave here. Some of you will take what you've learned back to our people in the occupied territory. Some of you will go on to other countries and wait for your instructions. But today we will celebrate, and tonight our leader will come here to give you his blessing. And then you will have your chance to demonstrate what you have learned for the man who made it possible."

*　*　*　*　*

The graduation ceremony was simple and unspectacular. Ahmed Tahril presented each of his new operatives with a month's pay followed by a proud embrace.

After the demonstration games there would be a fine dinner and the operatives would then be allowed to spend their last hours as they chose, the first free time they had been permitted in the eight weeks since their training began.

The demo-games would be carried out by three of the more advanced groups. Each group would consist of five to ten operatives. The balance of the trainees and the trainers would act as bystanders, hostages and the enemy troops.

Tahril was particularly enthusiastic about this group of young operatives. The major focus of their training had been suicide assaults, anti-rescue operations and aircraft hijacking and explosives placement.

Iraq had invested millions in this program. In exchange, it was agreed, Iraq would send its agents to the Providence camps for advanced training during the coming months.

The money had been well spent. An elaborate mock-up of a Boeing 747 had been constructed inside one of the huts, in order to avoid being photographed by satellites, and was used during training sessions. The Providence operatives were taught where to position their hostages in the hardest-to-reach areas of the aircraft so that any rescue attempt would, without a doubt, result in the death of those hostages.

Ahmed Tahril looked on with satisfaction as the demonstration progressed. Providence was growing, gaining more power. It would strike again and again in the homes and businesses and school yards of its enemies until the Western world was stunned into recognition. And the willingness to carry out attacks against symbolic and psychological targets was a weapon that could change the face of world politics.

* * * * *

Greg Abbott and three others arrived around four o'clock that afternoon. They were an odd group, Madison thought. There was Abbott in his perfectly creased pants and starched shirt. The chubby one they called Joe was jolly and pink and looked as if he had just been scrubbed. There was Charles, a small man with narrow little animal eyes, bony fingers and rumpled clothing. And the cook, a thick blonde named Margaret, who spoke German, understood little English, and disappeared into the kitchen immediately after her arrival. Madison had seen a dozen Margarets, both male and female, employed by Intelligence services to care for operatives and safe houses, experts at hearing and seeing nothing, professionals at becoming invisible.

The evening meal went as well as any meal could when five strangers sit down together and make an attempt at small talk. Margaret served stuffed flounder and did her best to avoid eye contact with anyone. Joe ate happily, Charles quietly, and Katherine rubbed her feet against Madison's under the table.

Halfway through the meal Abbott began

explaining to Madison, "Joe here is an expert in explosives preparation. He was part of the team that wrote the CIA field manuals on improvised explosives. Charles is an instructor at the Farm. We'll call his course self defense." He took a neat bite of his flounder and dabbed his lips with his napkin. "Katherine will brief you on the target's background and objectives. If you understand their goals you'll be better equipped in the field."

"And what is *your* function here, Abbott?" Madison inquired dryly, as each pair of eyes at the table looked at Greg Abbott.

Joe laughed aloud. "I was wondering the same thing. I noticed he brought his golf clubs along."

Greg Abbott smiled good-naturedly. "It's a nasty job but somebody's got to do it."

* * * * *

He was a giant of a man, standing over six feet, wide shoulders held straight. He tapped his pipe against the palm of his hand, crushed out the burning tobacco that fell to the concrete, and casually surveyed the street before entering the phone booth.

He could hear the distant clicks of the scrambling system that automatically began operation when this particular number was dialed. The call was answered at Mossad headquarters, Tel Aviv.

"I'm in," the big man reported with an obvious Irish brogue. "Met with Tahril last night. They've sent me and one of their operatives on a blasted shopping spree. We're buying portable radio-tape players. You know what that means. Some maniac will be carrying one of those things around loaded with plastic explosives. Sends chills up the spine, doesn't it?"

"We have information from a source in American Intelligence," said the Israeli agent. "The CIA is sending in one of their agents. A woman, unidentified as of yet. Keep your eyes open, and keep her out of the way."

"The Yanks do have a way of screwing up things, don't they, old son." The Irishman started to speak again but the sound of the glass door opening and the weight of a hand on his shoulder stopped him. He spun around to see Karl Speigel looking at him suspiciously.

"All right, old girl," he said into the receiver. "Good to talk to you again." He hung up.

"Who were you talking to?" Speigel demanded.

The big man wrapped his fingers around Speigel's wrist and removed the hand from his shoulder. "Listen up, Speigel, I don't need a bleedin' baby sitter. I'll not have it." He let go of the wrist and smiled slyly. "Just talkin' with a lady friend. Thought maybe I could find the time to stop in on her while I'm in Frankfurt."

Speigel studied him for a moment, searching the steady blue eyes. "Yes, perhaps I could meet this friend too," Speigel said.

The big man laughed and patted Speigel on the back. "That's it, lad. That's the spirit."

* * * * *

They were assigned separate work areas, depending on their requirements and methods. There was Katherine, who used the study off the living room which had been especially prepared for her with a sophisticated computer system. Katherine could sit in that dark room with its stuffed bookcases and deep leather chairs and access every documented piece of information available concerning the P.L.A.P. And there were times when Madison believed she had seen each and every document, every video tape and every photograph relating to the group and its leader. She had seen them, studied them until she knew them by heart, and listened to Katherine analyze them in her professional voice.

Madison had discovered that Katherine had different voices for different occasions. There was the one that laughed freely and perhaps a bit too loudly while Joe told his dirty jokes at dinner, the one that sounded as if it hadn't a care in the world after two glasses of red wine. Then there was the other voice, the one that spoke in whispered tones reserved for Madison's ears in the double bed of bedroom number four.

In her business voice she grilled Madison for three hours every day, warning her about the dangers of underestimating a man like Ahmed Tahril, a man who, unlike the stereotype of the terrorist leader, was neither ruled by emotion nor given to passionate displays.

"He is methodical and patient," she had told Madison. "He chooses his operatives carefully, using the more excitable and volatile ones for suicide assaults or publicity purposes. Because, as you know, nothing strikes fear in the heart of an American like seeing television footage of young people perfectly willing to die. The experienced commandos are used for planning and training and operations that require delicacy. Most of this group are simply paid killers who have no emotional involvement in the Palestinian cause at all."

There was the outgoing, pink-skinned Joe, who spent his assigned three hours a day with Madison in a small building off the main house, generally hovering over a sink with so much ease that he might have been preparing a cup of tea rather than some deadly potion. But Joe didn't seem at all burdened by the nature of his work. He taught Madison how to prepare plastic explosives, hand grenades and rocket launchers from ordinary household items, and readily explained their destructive power without a hint of restraint. He watched her mix up potassium chlorate and petroleum jelly as an explosive filler, watched her construct a homemade detonator from a light bulb and a cardboard toilet tissue tube, watched her mix in gunpowder, and praised her when she blew a hole the size of a man in the side of the building. Though he had said, as he was picking himself up and brushing himself off, that she may have used a bit too much of the powder.

And there was Charles, the small man with the narrow green eyes who preferred, when weather permitted, to do his work on a large exercise mat outside. He marched while he talked, circling Madison like a hunter, hands linked importantly behind his back, for, unlike Joe, Charles never took anything lightly. His grave little face peeked out at her from behind his protective mask as he worked on sharpening her offensive skills and made sure she could defend herself, kill, or sense the presence of a killer and react effectively without the benefit of a projectile weapon. He gave her a complete refresher course in the techniques of silent killing, instructing her patiently and warning her seriously of the responsibilities that came with knowing how to kill with the hands or with a manually utilized weapon. And even though Greg Abbott had politely referred to Charles as a self-defense specialist, Madison was well aware that he specialized in assassination techniques. "When you're in this type of situation," Charles had told her solemnly, "you've got to remain completely focused. No matter what is going on around you. In the mind of the trained killer, nothing else in the world exists except the target during those few seconds it takes to carry out the objective. It's his or her duty to locate and neutralize silently, and escape without being apprehended. It takes a great deal of skill and practice to live through this experience whether you're on the defensive or offensive side."

It was during the second week of training that Charles found it increasingly difficult to approach Madison without being seen or heard or felt. But it wasn't until she materialized in the dark hallway before dawn one morning when he was returning from the bathroom in his boxer shorts, and whispered "You're dead" in his ear, that Charles was sure Madison was ready for the field again.

And then there was Greg Abbott, who took Madison's morning runs with her and lectured her playfully on the evils of cigarettes even though she had covered the same distance in half the time. There was the Abbott who went from his jogging shorts straight into his perfectly creased slacks and polo shirts. Abbott who smiled diplomatically as he disengaged himself gracefully from the dinner table and went to the study where he made his hushed telephone reports to an anonymous official. Abbott who laughed and joked and relaxed because he believed Madison needed to take time to laugh and joke and relax. Abbott who never lost his focus, whose central concern always seemed to be Madison. Abbott who tried so hard to show her that he was a reliable man because he knew her confidence and trust was as important to the operation as her training. Madison wished him more ease. Still she was grateful for his conscientiousness.

During the day Greg Allen Abbott, ever mindful of Madison's conditioning, strode the grounds like an anxious proprietor, occasionally dropping in on her and Joe or sticking his lean face in the study door to see how the briefing sessions were going with Katherine, ever mindful of Madison's conditioning. And at night he insisted that they all rest and relax, and told Madison that absolutely no work would be done in the evenings.

And with each passing day Madison grew to trust and respect her preparation team, and when there were only two days remaining on the island, she suddenly realized that she would miss these people with whom she had shared living quarters, meals, morning runs and anecdotes. She would miss seeing Charles with his little legs crossed under him in the morning while he meditated. And Joe when he launched into some ridiculous monologue over dinner that kept them shaking their heads and laughing. And Katherine, and all her voices. And Abbott:

There would be plenty more of Abbott in her future. He was her controller, her lifeline.

* * * * *

It was nearly midnight when Greg Abbott walked into the study and found Katherine sitting in front of the computer, Madison's file on the screen. The word "Classified" blinked menacingly in the top left hand corner. He put his hand on Katherine's shoulder gently. "You've done a good job, Maloane. She's as ready as she'll ever be."

Startled at first by his sudden appearance, Katherine spun around, but recovered quickly. "I can't believe it's been three weeks already. I keep wondering if I've left something out."

Abbott sat down. "Checking out her file, huh? That should make you feel better abut sending her out there. As you can see, she's a very capable woman."

"Do you think she really realizes how dangerous this assignment could be?"

"Madison is no stranger to dangerous assignments." He reached over and turned Katherine's swivel chair towards him. "Let me tell you something about our new friend Madison that you won't find in her file. She's a killer, Katherine. I've talked to people who have worked with her in the field. She's a natural, she's got the instincts for it. That's why we chose her."

CHAPTER FIVE

Terry Woodall stood on the deck of her beach house staring absently at the water. Spring was early this year. She could feel the warmth in the wet air and the heat from a newly risen sun as it burned through the clouds and promised a hot day.

She had been up for hours and, in truth, she couldn't have said how long she had been standing there, letting her thoughts stray, watching the turbulent morning water crash against the beach. Suddenly she turned and walked back into the house. She went to the telephone and pressed Marge

Price's home number, checking her watch as it rang. Six forty-five a.m.

"Yes?"

"Marge, it's Terry. Listen, I have to get in touch with Madison. I've made a terrible mistake. I don't care what she wants to do, or who she wants to work for. It doesn't matter. I just want her back. I need her, Marge. I can't think about anything else. I miss her so badly. I —"

"Terry," Marge broke in hesitantly. "Madison left yesterday."

"Oh, God. Where?"

"All I know is she's out of the country. I don't know if I can even get a message to her now . . . I'm sorry."

"How could I have let her go like that? I may never see her again. I may never have another chance to tell her I'm sorry."

"Don't be silly. She'll be back," Marge answered with as much assurance as she could assemble.

"Thanks, Marge," Terry said quietly, replacing the receiver and lowering herself slowly into a chair. She sat there silently for several minutes, and then muttered, "What have I done?"

* * * * *

Later that evening in Washington, D.C., Katherine Maloane walked into the Comedy Cafe and ordered a glass of wine. Katherine was no stranger to 1520 K Street. She had been coming to the Friday night show on and off for nearly a year.

Earlier that day she had left her condominium porch light burning. It was the signal she used to let her Soviet controller know when she had some bit of Intelligence to pass along.

When the first show ended, Katherine paid her tab and left a folded sheet of paper lying under the ashtray. She never stayed long enough to see who picked up the notes, and she never inquired as to how the Intelligence was processed. For the next few mornings Katherine would walk the last four blocks to work and look for a single orange chalk mark on a certain Pennsylvania Avenue telephone pole. It was the code that told her to stop by a local cafe at exactly seven a.m. the next day to retrieve her commission, five to twenty-five thousand dollars depending on the importance of the Intelligence she had delivered. There was always a different face waiting in the cafe to brush past her and casually drop, on the seat beside her, the envelope containing money and a list of detailed questions. Sometimes the items of interest to the Soviets would be as simple as embassy floor plans in Europe. At other times, however, Katherine Maloane, Soviet code name Bluebird, had provided detailed information concerning State Department sentiment towards current arms agreements, which would naturally aid the Soviets in the arms reduction talks, provide them with limits, tell them on which points the American government might show flexibility. She had also provided them with the names of American agents working under diplomatic cover. For each name she received a minimum of twenty thousand dollars.

* * * * *

Madison flew into Frankfurt am Main and passed through customs without complication. Her passport listed her name as Gretchen Zahn, an American writer visiting relatives in West Germany. Outside the airport, she flagged a taxi. *"Zum Hauptbahnhof, bitte,"* she instructed the driver, knowing her first stop must be the train station.

The day was overcast, as is often the case in Frankfurt, and Madison peered intently through the window as the taxi rushed through the city streets of Germany's financial capital. There was a vitality about Frankfurt, an informality Madison sensed every time she was there. The city had disengaged itself from the burden of its past, and become a rebuilt, modern city of soaring, glittering towers, powerful banks, and luxury hotels.

As the taxi passed over the River Main, Madison rolled down the window and took a deep breath. A new city, a new identity. Somehow it was always so much easier pretending to be someone else.

Madison saw the Hauptbahnhof on the next block and instructed the driver to drop her off at the corner of Mannheimerstrasse. She walked less than a block, suitcase in hand, to the train station carpark where she found what she had come for, an automobile which had been leased a few days prior to her arrival in the name of Gretchen Zahn. The cream colored Mercedes-Benz would attract little attention: there were hundreds just like it in the city.

Opening the glove box, she found a sheet of paper which listed the address of an apartment that had been rented for her, a door key taped to the paper. She reached behind the front seat and smiled when she found the two bags Abbott had promised would be there. One held a CO_2 pistol, a pair of Zeiss night vision binoculars, blasting caps, gunpowder and a German made Sig-Sauer 226, 9mm semi-automatic pistol with a silencer. The second bag held twenty-five thousand dollars, half of which had already been converted into West German marks.

She checked under the seat and found an AK-47 assault rifle. Madison studied the weapon suspiciously. This was not a weapon used in self-defense. Its purpose was killing, and Madison had not been sent to Frankfurt to kill. She stuffed the rifle back under the seat, hoping she would not have to use it, and started the engine. Her next stop would be her new residence, Bockenheimer 17, Frankfurt.

Only yards away from where Madison's vehicle pulled out of the carpark, Yuri Vissarionovich Kaski climbed into his automobile and laid his binoculars on the seat next to him. The Soviet agent smiled. "It has been a long time, Scorpion. But I have not forgotten."

* * * * *

Madison nodded in pleasure when she parked in front of her new address. She had assumed it would be an inexpensive flat or room in the seedy section of town. She had stayed in so many little run-down dumps over the years — rooms with peeling paint and yellowed sheets, flats with creaky stairs and leaking roofs. But what she found here was a lovely row of townhouses nestled together facing a well-kept courtyard.

Inside the three-story townhouse she found long, narrow rooms and arched ceilings with heavy wood beams reaching from wall to wall. The kitchen and dining area were on ground level, the living and recreation rooms on the second floor, two bedrooms with baths on the third.

After unpacking a few items and carefully placing the bags with the weapons and money under the bed, Madison hurried to the kitchen. She had been far too preoccupied to eat on the plane and now the rumbling in her stomach reminded her that she had not had any food since leaving the United States.

The kitchen was fully stocked, and Madison gratefully chose sausage and gherkins, white cheese and a glass of Ebbelwei, the apple wine of the region and a favorite of Madison's. Halfway through her dinner she checked her watch, and hurriedly slid her plate aside.

"You're late," Abbott answered without bothering to say hello.

"I know. I'm afraid I'm a bit out of the practice of keeping schedules."

"Better get in the practice right away. You've got twenty-four hours to relax and then you'll make your Frankfurt debut. The target is the Dresdner Bank. No one is to get hurt. It'll be after hours so all you'll have to deal with are two security guards. We want lots of smoke, very little fire. Understand? Not so much damage that the bank can't be operational again. It's a German bank but it has a considerable amount of American interest behind it. The next day we'll have someone call our embassy and claim credit for the bombing, saying it was directed at American interests and carried out by a former CIA operative. After a couple of strikes like that you'll be pretty popular. Providence will take the bait. Just be damned sure you stay out of the way of the authorities. They'll be just as anxious to find you as Providence. You're going to have to be visible but not obvious."

"Got it."

"By the way," Abbott went on with a grin in his voice, "how do you like the accommodations?"

Madison smiled. "Quite acceptable actually. And not at all what I expected. Don't tell me you did all this for me."

"Well, we have to maintain the illusion of being respectable, don't we?" Abbott joked. "It's leased in the name of an American publishing house. You're their guest there." He paused. "How are you doing? Getting adjusted all right?"

"Doing fine, Greg. It's all coming back to me. Haven't been away that long, you know."

He smiled. Madison had never used his first name. It had always been either Abbott or Mr. Abbott, and it had always kept them at a distance. He was glad for the familiarity.

"This will be the last time you call me from that number. Pay phones from now on. You'll call the local number I gave you to get your instructions, starting day after tomorrow at nine a.m. And don't be late this time. Any questions?"

"No questions."

Greg Abbott hung up and looked at the Director of Central Intelligence. "No problems. No questions."

Mitchell Colby smiled. "You've done a good job,

Greg. Now let's see what kind of job our secret weapon will do. And let's hope to God she can do it without getting herself killed."

CHAPTER SIX

A sound . . . Madison opened her eyes and automatically reached for the gun under her pillow, screwed on the silencer, and checked to be sure the magazine was in place. Another sound . . . It was from no part of the city beyond the townhouse walls. Madison stepped out of bed and silently slipped into her jeans, her heart rate increasing.

Then, the sound again . . . A door creaking, a footstep downstairs. Moving to the door, her back against the wall, she leaned her head through and saw a shadow, dark, imposing. Someone on the lower level. A man, a weapon in his hand, had moved quietly past the window, briefly illuminated by the lights from the street. Madison took a deep, hushed breath, then darted across the hall to the top of the stairs and started down the staircase slowly, defensively, her senses alert for any sound, any movement.

Suddenly the quiet spit of a silenced weapon sliced the air. The man had fired from the bottom of the stairs. There was no defense. Madison made her body arch, made herself let out a groan as she collapsed on the landing, willing her pulse rate to slow, her breathing to stop, the gun clutched in her right hand.

He took one step at a time, moving carefully, the plush carpet crushing under his dark shoes, the automatic weapon pointing at her. He reached the landing and squatted, placing one clammy hand on her neck to check for a pulse. Madison crashed the pistol into his face and sent him reeling backwards down the stairs. But he had the quickness and agility of a professional and in an instant had regained control and slipped into the shadows.

The 9mm in her hands, Madison took each step cautiously, her back pressed against the wall, her mind going over the layout of the first floor. There was a sofa, chairs, tables, a bookcase, and a door off to the left that was the kitchen.

She reached the last step, then crouched and rolled into the living room, working her way behind the couch, the quiet pops of the assassin's pistol digging up the carpet behind her.

Then his dark outline passed across the doorway. He was out of position now, Madison realized. He had moved in hopes of catching a glimpse of her and in the process had put himself on the wrong side of the door. He would be forced to lean forward or cross again, exposing himself for one crucial second.

Then it happened. He darted across the doorway. Madison fired. She heard the air rush out of his body like a low, quiet cough, heard the thud on the tiled floor. She was there in a second, her semi-automatic pressing into his back as he lay face down, her other hand groping for the light switch.

She saw his weapon lying next to him and kicked it out of reach, then rolled him over. "Yuri," she whispered, astounded.

He opened his eyes slowly. "I never forget my enemies," said the Soviet agent.

"Don't tell me you're still upset over that nasty business in Zurich," Madison said softly as she hovered over him.

Barely conscious, Kaski whispered with a heavy Russian accent, "You nearly ruined my career. It wasn't so important to you. Your position was stable. You pursued me because you wanted to prove that you are better."

"It was my job, Yuri Vissarionovich. You were about to carry a briefcase full of my country's secrets back to the Soviet Union."

Yuri Vissarinovich Kaski studied her silently, his hazel eyes weak. Madison dabbed the perspiration from his forehead with a kitchen towel. "The cold war is supposed to be over, my old friend," she said gently.

The Russian gave her a half smile. "And if you believe that, Scorpion, you are not as brilliant as you think you are."

"How did you find me?" Madison asked, but he did not answer. His eyes, locked on hers, were frozen, the stare lifeless.

* * * * *

By dawn she had called the local number, reported the incident and arranged for a local team to pick up the dead Russian's body from the townhouse. She showered and changed into faded jeans and a jeans jacket, pulled the thick auburn hair back and placed a pair of wire rimmed glasses on her small, straight nose before stepping out into the fine morning mist.

The shops would not open for another hour, so Madison made use of the time by driving past the Dresdner Bank and studying the structure from her automobile. It was a large building with two levels and a predominantly glass front. She quickly formulated her plan of attack. She parked her car and walked to a small cafe, where she ordered her breakfast in perfect German, and tossed the plan round in her mind until it seemed as structurally sound as the Dresdner Bank.

An hour later she stepped onto the busy sidewalk, letting the crowds move her, flowing with them as if she had followed this particular routine every day of her life. She purchased a pair of black sweatpants, a black sweatshirt, and black sneakers. On her next stop she bought a dark rinse for her hair. At a hardware store she found double-sided tape, velcro, a six-inch iron pipe with threaded ends, two pipe screw caps, and pliers. Not your ordinary shopping list, she thought as she walked to the Mercedes.

It was not until she was loading the bags into the back seat that she felt something was wrong, something in the crowd. Madison had been trained to feel the rhythm of the street, to sense the odd footstep, to know when the flow had been disturbed. A silent alarm sounded in her mind . . . Someone was following her.

Calmly, she closed the car, locked it and returned to the sidewalk. Standing in front of a shop window, she saw the reflection of a woman behind her, suddenly still, a newspaper in her hand. Madison walked several yards, turned sharply and saw the woman glance at a dark van pulling away from the curb. Madison looked at the van then back at the woman.

"Damn you, Abbott, you bloody fool," she muttered and quickly walked to a call box.

Greg Abbott answered the private line in his State Department office. "Madison? What are you talking about?"

"You know what I'm talking about. You've got a rookie agent on me that any idiot could spot in a crowd and an entire listening post trailing only yards behind. If you want to advertise my presence here why don't I just wear a sandwich board around my neck?"

Abbott laughed. "They're there to be sure you're safe, not to obstruct you in any way. After you reported the trouble with Kaski we thought you'd be better off with some protection. Their orders are to stay well back."

"Cancel their orders."

Abbott ignored her demands. "I've been going over your files all night. You and Kaski had a history, I see. We've got a leak somewhere, Madison, or he would never have found you."

Madison sighed. "Brilliant deductive skills, Abbott."

"If the KGB knows, the whole operation is blown. They'll leak it to Providence. They'd like nothing better than to have one of our operations blow up in our face."

"I'm not convinced they know about the operation. In fact, I'm not even convinced that Yuri made a report to KGB headquarters. He was the senior Intelligence officer here. He may have just decided to deal with me himself. Kaski was like that. He vowed to kill me years ago, he just couldn't let go of it. God, what a waste." She paused. "Anyway, I really think the operation is still safe, but you've got to call off the surveillance. It's too obvious. Providence would be able to spot them right away."

"I'll have them back off a little," Abbott suggested.

"*No,*" Madison said, raising her voice. "If you want this to work, you'll let me handle this alone. We have no choice."

Greg Allen Abbott was silent for a few seconds, and then in a defeated tone he answered, "All right. I'll pull them out."

Madison turned and looked at the woman, who was studiously not looking at her, then spoke angrily into the receiver. "And, please, don't do anything like this again without consulting me first. It's my rear on the line out here. I'm dead if I'm exposed. You should know that."

Madison replaced the receiver and leaned against the inside of the phone booth. Minutes later she saw the van disappearing around the corner. The woman who had been shadowing her was nowhere in sight. Greg Abbott had wasted no time. She breathed a sigh of relief and walked in the direction of her car. There was one more stop to make before returning to the townhouse.

An hour later, after darkening her hair with the brown rinse, Madison sat on the bedroom floor unpacking the items she had purchased earlier. A compact disk quietly played Chopin in the background. The music always seemed to calm her, help her focus. It had been strange walking into the townhouse alone again. Some part of her had half-expected to hear Terry's voice, or see her walking in the front door, smiling, a bag of groceries in her arms. It's the small things you do with a partner, she thought, like unpacking groceries or listening to music, that you miss the most.

She remembered Elicia, the lover she had spent five years with in England, the woman who had been murdered, shot down in the streets of London. Madison, knowing that she had been the intended target, had never quite reconciled her feelings about Elicia, a vibrant, caring woman who knew the dangers and still loved her totally. Madison had carried the guilt with her ever since that tragic day.

And then there was Terry, young, beautiful, complicated. A woman with whom she had fallen deeply in love, in perhaps the worst time of her life. She had still been dealing with the loss of Elicia when she and Terry had met, but the attraction between them could not be denied. And Terry, understanding what Elicia had brought to Madison's life, had let her keep her good memories, was unthreatened by them, and helped her fight the bad ones. Madison remembered their summer chats on the beach when Terry had told her it was perfectly fine to be in love with the memory of Elicia, and then stated flatly that she thought she loved Elicia too. She remembered grabbing Terry and hugging her that day, remembered how they swore themselves to each other, remembered trying to make love in the sand and laughing when they both admitted it was very impractical.

Smiling to herself, Madison reached under the bed for the bags. It was time to put some of the skills she had learned on the island into practice.

She began with a blasting cap and a fuse cord, using her pliers to tighten the cap over the fuse. She then attached a screw cap to one end of the iron pipe and partially filled the pipe with black powder, dropped the blasting cap and fuse inside, and filled the remaining space with more powder. Fingers moving with precision and skill, Madison McGuire constructed what was commonly known as a pipe grenade in less than a half hour. The balance of the work to be done on the explosive was simply a matter of securing the pipe grenade to the small wooden block she had purchased on her last stop and then attaching it to a narrow wooden push rod which could be inserted into the end of a rifle. The grenade was rough and unsophisticated but it would serve its purpose, and most importantly, the material she had used could not be traced back to the U.S.

Government. It must appear that she was working completely alone.

She checked her watch. Barely noon. The operation would not begin until at least ten that evening. It was the waiting that had always disturbed her most about the job, the long, unbearable hours of inactivity. She leaned back on the floor and closed her eyes . . .

The waiting began.

* * * * *

She dressed slowly, her mind churning. She tucked the sweatshirt into the black pants and wrapped the belt around her waist. Then, she cut several pieces, no longer than two inches, from the double-sided tape and attached them to the belt. A small strip of velcro was then applied to the tape, the Zeiss binoculars, and the CO_2 pistol so that each item could be fastened to her belt and not be a hindrance if she needed to move quickly. She stuffed the 9mm Sig-Sauer into the back of her pants, zipped up the dark jacket, and jogged across the room to be sure all the equipment was secure and noiseless. Sure that she was prepared, Madison walked downstairs, pulled a bottle of scotch from a dining room cabinet, and drained a short glass, neat. It was time to move, at last.

* * * * *

The bank was dark, the inside lights turned off hours ago. Madison had been parked across from the bank for over an hour, the night vision binoculars trained on the glass-fronted building. Abbott's Intelligence had been correct, apparently. There seemed to be only two guards inside. She had seen them pass in front of the windows.

Several yards away in a cream-colored van, two men sat watching her. "Who is she?" asked one of them. "You think she's part of the security?"

"I'm not sure," answered Karl Speigel, Providence's top West German operative. "But she's in the way. We'll have to take her out first."

"Wait," the other man said, as Karl Speigel withdrew his weapon. "She's getting out. Jesus, that's no security guard, Karl."

"Quick, get the camera," Speigel ordered.

* * * * *

Madison zigzagged down the block and across the street, keeping low to the ground. At the corner of the bank she crouched briefly to catch her breath. She had to get the attention of the guards inside without alarming them. Above all they mustn't suspect any threat to the bank or they would set off the alarm. Her only chance was to draw them out, away from the lobby so they wouldn't be harmed. It had worked with Yuri Vissarionovich Kaski, she thought; the same kind of deception might work with the bank guards.

She took off the belt and then pulled the band from her hair, letting her hair drop to her shoulders. She stepped just in front of the window, in view of the guards inside, affected an expression of panic, banged on the window, then suddenly dropped to the sidewalk out of sight and crawled to the corner of the bank.

Seconds later she heard the door open, heard a female voice call out in German, "She is hurt."

Then footsteps coming towards her: one guard had come out of the bank. When the guard was almost on her she sat up and fired the CO_2 pistol. The hypodermic needle embedded itself in the female guard's leg. The drug began doing its job within seconds— the guard wavered and then slowly dropped. Madison quickly pulled her around the corner and out of sight of the second guard.

Perhaps sixty seconds later she heard a male voice call out for his partner. Madison waited at the corner of the building, and when the guard stepped in front of her she brought the butt of her pistol down on the base of his neck.

The two men inside the van exchanged astonished glances as Madison coolly returned the belt to her waist, attached the empty CO_2 pistol, and started back across the street, the 9mm pistol in her hand.

To Madison's horror, she heard another voice call out in German, ordering her to stop. *Oh shit, there's a third guard.*

Madison did not stop. She could not let herself be taken in for questioning.

The loud report from a pistol echoed through the streets. The bullet creased Madison's left arm. She spun around and hit the pavement rolling, then fired her automatic. The guard dropped, a dark pool of blood quickly forming around him.

She stood up, holding her left arm, feeling the

warm blood running between her fingers, and looked at the man lying on the sidewalk in front of the bank. Then, sirens in the distance. Someone had seen or heard, someone had called the police. She crossed the street quickly, reached into the car and shoved the wooden push rod into the rifle barrel, lit the fuse and fired at the bank, shattering the glass front. A split second later the homemade grenade went off, fire erupted inside the bank and an ear-splitting alarm sounded. The sirens close now, Madison jumped in her car praying she could get out in time. She drove slowly, not wanting to attract attention, her arm on fire with pain.

The cream-colored van raced out of the parking lot. The driver, an American, turned to Karl Speigel. "Holy shit. What was that all about? Who the hell is she?"

"I do not know, my friend. But I intend to find out why she did the job for us," Speigel answered.

* * * * *

Madison returned to the townhouse and entered as quietly as possible, not wanting to be seen by the neighbors. She dressed the arm as best she could, relieved to find that it would not require medical care. Then she went upstairs and fell back on the bed. She had done it, pulled off her first assignment in over a year, but an innocent man had been shot in the process.

"Blast," she said, sitting up, running her hands through her hair, trying to push away the questions in her mind. Could she have handled it differently? No, she told herself, there was no time to aim for an arm or leg, and if there had been, he might have fired again. She wondered if he would live, if he had a family, wondered if there were children or a wife who would get the call in the night.

She found the bottle of scotch, knowing all too well why so many intelligence agents had drinking problems. But tonight she didn't care, she just needed a drink.

CHAPTER SEVEN

It was nearly two a.m. before the photographs were developed and enlarged at Providence's Frankfurt headquarters, a three-room flat strewn with newspapers, mounds of paperwork, maps, radios and computers. Three people stood at a small round table and studied the photographs.

One of the three was Michael Peelor, a former member of the U.S. Delta antiterrorist force, who had dropped out of sight some years ago after he had watched eight of his fellow soldiers be burned alive at Desert One in a failed mission known as

Operation Rice Bowl, which had been designed to rescue the hostages held in Tehran. Something had snapped in Peelor that day. He had seen men die before, had even watched friends die, but he hadn't been prepared for the terrible ride back to the States on that day in 1980.

The C-141 transport plane had been filled with the Delta survivors who sat there silently, unable to look at one another. They had dreamed of this day, dreamed of the victorious ride home with the freed hostages. They would have been heroes. Instead, after several mechanical failures the mission, which they had trained for for five long months, had been aborted. And then, the unthinkable had happened: A terrible dust storm at the desert landing area two hundred miles southeast of Tehran, causing a government helicopter to collide with a C-130 plane preparing for takeoff. Eight soldiers had been killed and another five seriously burned. The survivors returned to the States failures, the full frustration of the American people unfairly thrust on them. They were not welcomed as heroes, they were ridiculed as incompetents. Michael Peelor, his need to be successful greater than the need to serve his country, left Delta Force and put himself on the international market, a soldier of fortune. Providence quickly snapped him up. He now spent most of his time as an operative trainer between Frankfurt and Lebanon's Bekaa Valley.

The other two standing at the table were Karl Speigel, Ahmed Tahril's top operative, and a young Israeli woman.

Yael Chazan was in her early twenties, but dark eyes and black hair gave her a sharp, almost severe bearing. Yael's family had been sympathetic to the Palestinian cause, a sentiment not shared by most Israelis or Jewish settlers in Israel. This openness, learned from her family, caused Yael to join a women's group known as Women In Black. Every Friday the women met, dressed in black, at a busy Tel Aviv intersection, holding signs which read, END THE OCCUPATION. One of these Fridays Yael met and eventually fell in love with Rafik Ashrawi, an intense young Palestinian radical, who finally met his end in the occupied territory of the Gaza Strip.

Yael, full of grief and anger, became increasingly frustrated with the approach taken by Women In Black and began to speak openly about taking part in radical acts in order to end the occupation. A Providence operative, hearing of the young, outspoken Israeli woman, contacted and eventually recruited her. She was trained in the camps of the Bekaa Valley and quickly proved herself to be a dedicated and effective operative.

Karl Speigel looked at Michael Peelor and Yael Chazan. "Do either of you recognize this woman?" Both Chazan and Peelor shook their heads. "Well, she's obviously a professional. I'll fax this photograph to Libyan Intelligence."

Michael Peelor pushed the unkempt shoulder-length hair away from his face. "Ask the Irishman. He's been around for a while."

Speigel, who had an instinctive distrust of Providence's new explosives man, turned and called to the back room. "Max, come here, please."

The big Irishman walked into the room brightly, twisting up the corners of his bushy mustache. "Ever seen this woman?" Speigel asked, shoving a photograph of Madison McGuire under Max Rudger's nose.

"Holy Mother of God," Max Rudger blurted.

The other three exchanged glances. "Who is she?" Yael inquired.

Max Rudger's mind was reeling. He had just seen a photograph of a very dear friend in the hands of Providence operatives. And what in hell was she doing? And what would he say now? He looked up at Speigel. "Where did this come from?"

"Outside the Dresdner Bank. We never got the chance to use your bomb because this woman launched a frigging grenade in the lobby."

"But not before she silenced two guards, shot one right in front of the bank, got clipped in the arm and then launched the grenade." Michael Peelor added with frank admiration, "It was fantastic."

Max tried to hide his relief. He knew Madison, knew how she operated, knew that if she had not wanted to be seen she would not have been seen. The question was, whose attention was she trying to draw? Suddenly he realized that she must be the American agent Israeli Intelligence had told him about, the American sent to infiltrate Providence.

"Her name is McGuire, Madison McGuire. She's a former CIA field agent. Saw her in London last year, just before she hung it up."

"She is a friend of yours?" Yael asked.

Max nodded. "Met her in Ireland several years ago when I was leaving the IRA. One of the best agents you've ever laid your eyes on, she was. Ice cold sometimes too. You just never knew with Madison. She's like a blasted pendulum swinging from light to dark with no warning."

"Why haven't I ever heard of her?" Peelor asked.

Max smiled. "Top secret stuff, you know. Always went by a code name. Disguises herself too. Could be the professional next door, the bag lady in the street, anyone, anywhere. She's all pro. This is the Scorpion, my friends. Name sound familiar?"

"Holy shit," Peelor answered, drawing the picture closer to his face.

* * * * *

Madison found a call box and dialed her contact number.

"Identify, please," answered the benign voice on the other end.

"McGuire, Madison," was her reply.

"No operational instructions at this time. Please ring again at two p.m."

Madison sighed. As she turned to leave the telephone booth, her attention was suddenly and strangely drawn to a passing limousine. Then it happened. The explosion was deafening.

Madison instinctively hit the ground, covering her head as smoldering hot pieces of metal flew in all directions. There were screams from the crowd, burned bodies lying helpless on the other side of the street, the sickening smell of gasoline and burning flesh. Then another car that had been too close to the limo slammed into a nearby telephone pole, its windshield shattering, its gas tank leaking. The occupants climbed out and attempted to crawl away, too shaken by the incredible series of events to move quickly. Madison darted into the street and grabbed the woman first, pulling with all her strength to get her out of the way before the second automobile exploded.

The woman was limp, dazed. Madison dragged her onto the sidewalk.

"Keep your head down. Cover your eyes," she ordered in German. The driver, bleeding from the crash, his pants ripped to the thigh, was attempting to crawl away, his right leg dragging behind him.

Madison looked at the automobile and then at the pavement under it, wet with gasoline, knowing only seconds remained. She dashed into the street and grabbed his arm, wrapped it around her shoulders, struggling to get him onto his feet, feeling her shirtsleeve begin to moisten with blood from the bullet wound in her arm. He was a large man, and Madison, though strong, was not a large woman. Breathing hard, sweat running from her hairline, she summoned every bit of force in her to get him to the other side of the street.

They were near the sidewalk when the sparks reached the stream of gasoline escaping from the automobile. The impact of the explosion was so great both Madison and the man were thrown to the ground. Madison rolled several feet, her jeans splitting at the knees, blood trickling from skinned elbows. The man crawled to his female partner and they held each other, both sobbing, the man too stunned to realize that his leg had been broken. When the couple looked up to find the woman who had pulled them to safety, she was nowhere in sight.

* * * * *

"Is this your idea of keeping a low profile?" Greg Abbott shouted furiously when Madison made contact later that afternoon. "What the hell were you doing? Some idiot with a video camera got the whole rescue on tape and now CNN is showing the footage every thirty minutes."

"I know," Madison answered quietly. "The afternoon papers just hit the street with my photograph on the front page. I tossed the glasses and washed the rinse out of my hair. I also did some shopping and bought clothes that look a bit more professional. No one will recognize me now."

"Did you know that the female security guard recognized the picture and phoned the authorities? They don't know what to make of it . . . Jesus, Madison, how could you let this happen?" Abbott demanded.

"My dear Abbott," Madison answered slowly, running short on patience, "what in bloody hell was I supposed to do? Let those people fry in the street? By the way, I wasn't badly hurt."

"I just can't get a handle on you. You take out a Soviet agent, put a bullet through a guard's chest, and then risk everything to save two strangers."

Madison fell silent for a few moments. She could offer no real explanation. She had acted on impulse. "Who was in the limo? The papers aren't releasing any names yet."

"His name was Wilhelm Dhom. He was on the board of the Dresdner Bank."

"Oh, no," Madison muttered more to herself than to Abbott.

"Oh, yes," he countered. "Of course you realize what this means. The authorities think you're responsible. It's the only good thing to come out of this mess. We can use this, Madison. It fits in perfectly with our plans. Providence will know you mean business."

"What if Providence is responsible for the bombing?"

"Even better. They won't like you stealing their thunder. They'll be even more determined to find you."

"Great," Madison answered, leaning back against the phone booth, lighting a cigarette. "Why don't I feel all together good about that?"

"You can handle it. If you'll try and avoid the heroics everything will work out just fine . . . By the way, your orders are to clear out of the townhouse. Someone could have seen you going in and out. They may recognize the picture in the paper."

"Done already. I took everything out and wiped the place down right after the explosion. I'm at the Frankfurter Hof."

Abbott laughed. "Frankfurter Hof, huh? Well, we certainly have a knack for spending government money, don't we?"

"It's just part of the cover. The hotel is filled with business types and with the right clothes it's easy enough to blend in." She added, "By the way, I dumped the car just in case someone saw it, and I'm using the alternate I.D. you gave me, so if you have to contact me I'm listed as Lilian Guth, room three-one-seven."

"Listen, I think it's best if you lay low for a couple of days."

"I'm grateful for that. Don't think I've had a full night's sleep since I got here."

"Call the local number day after tomorrow at nine and get your new orders . . . And Madison, try and stay out of trouble."

Madison smiled. "It will be my pleasure."

* * * * *

"What do you know about her?" Ahmed Tahril demanded, as he looked at the photographs of Madison McGuire that Karl Speigel gave him inside Libya's military intelligence headquarters in Tripoli.

"Her name is Madison McGuire, code name Scorpion. She —"

"This is Scorpion?" Tahril interrupted, holding the photographs closer now, studying them carefully. "It was my understanding she had retired."

"They retired her last year after a failed operation. Our sources tell us the CIA lost track of her within weeks. She never showed up for the debriefings, went underground."

Ahmed Tahril looked out of the glass-walled office into the heart of the agency. Rows of men and women sat in a long, narrow room behind computers and radios, some wearing headphones, some frantically scribbling notes on yellow pads, others punching computer keyboards. He stared at Speigel, the photographs still clutched in his hand. "And now she shows up in Frankfurt. It is very suspicious. I want all the information you can get on her. She's after something. Perhaps it is us she wants."

The head of Libyan Intelligence walked in and

set a file down in front of Tahril in time to catch the last part of the conversation. He was a short, thin man with dark hair and eyes, wearing the khaki uniform of his country and a pistol on his hip.

"Under normal circumstances I would agree with you, Ahmed," he said. "But we have run a complete history, and drained all our sources. This woman may have been CIA at one time, but no more. Whatever she's doing, whatever motivates her, has little to do with the American government."

"And you are sure the information is accurate?" Tahril asked.

"Oh, yes, Ahmed. We have gone so far as to get classified material. On the surface the CIA will not even admit that this agent ever existed. However, their files tell a very different story."

Ahmed Tahril reached for the file and began scanning it at once. Twenty minutes later he closed the file and looked at the Intelligence officer. "Whatever she is doing may have *everything* to do with the American government. It looks as if the Americans did not deal with her fairly, my friends. In that capacity we have something in common. Perhaps we can make her an offer more to her liking." He turned to his operative. "Karl, find this woman and bring her to me. It seems a shame to have such talent ignored."

"And if she does not agree to come?"

"It is not open for debate. I will make arrangements to fly to Frankfurt. Meet me there and bring the woman."

* * * * *

89

Max Rudger, finding himself temporarily free from the watchful eyes of Karl Speigel, set out alone early in the morning dressed in the only suit and tie he owned. He purchased a guide to Frankfurt hotels, then, seeing that the morning was mild and the first signs of spring had arrived, decided to treat himself to breakfast at a pavement cafe near the River Main.

With strong German coffee steaming by his elbow, Max scribbled down the names of several hotels. Knowing Madison would choose an expensive hotel where the authorities would be less likely to search for her, he narrowed his list down to three hotels, the Canadian Pacific Frankfurt Plaza, a plush new luxury hotel, the Frankfurt Inter-Continental which offered a view of the Main and the Frankfurt skyline, and the Frankfurt Hof, an old restored hotel that once served as Allied headquarters.

He chose the Inter-Continental first, and tipped the desk clerk two hundred Deutsche marks for a discreet look at the guest register. Several of the rooms held female occupants, and Max, having no idea what name Madison might be using, committed the names and room numbers to memory and began his surveillance. Two hours later he had seen the occupants of those rooms either going in or coming out. He moved on to the Frankfurt Plaza where the desk clerk was so uncooperative that he was forced to leave or be thrown out.

His next stop was the Frankfurt Hof where he found the narrow-eyed clerk surly and curt but very willing to be persuaded, providing the price was right. After some hostile negotiation, Max managed a look at the register. It was going to be a long day.

He tried the restaurant first, then sat in the lobby reading the newspaper, occasionally looking at the clerk who had agreed to nod when one of his female guests entered the lobby or dropped off a key at the front desk, as is customary in European hotels. Within another two hours the field was narrowed to two names, Lilian Guth, room three-seventeen and Norma Roth, room eleven-forty.

He tried Norma Roth first, for no other reason than he liked the name. He posted himself in the hallway and waited. After nearly another hour without anyone leaving the room he became impatient and decided to risk a knock on the door. An elderly woman answered with rollers in her tinted hair and a mud mask on her face. Max, feeling very foolish and a bit embarrassed, apologized and made his way to the third floor. With a sigh he approached room three-seventeen and knocked on the door.

"Yes?" a voice answered hesitantly.

It's Madison. By God I've found her. Max leaned against the door and spoke just loud enough for her to hear. "Put the blasted gun down and open the door, old girl. Busted my ass and spent nearly every mark I had tryin' to find you."

On those words the door flew open. "Max, what are you doing here?" Madison wrapped her arms around his big neck and gave him a kiss on the cheek.

"I should ask you the same question," he said, and plopped himself on the bed. "Have you seen the news, read the papers today? Good Christ, woman, haven't you learned how to do anything quietly in all these years?"

Madison laughed and stepped back, looking him up and down. "I must say, old man, we're looking quite distinguished these days."

"Tryin' to change the subject, are you?" He jabbed one long finger in her direction. "You listen to me Madi McGuire, you might have gone too far this time. And where in the hell is Terry? Don't tell me you've gone and botched up that one too."

"I'm afraid so," Madison responded quietly, walking to a table by the window and pouring two cups of coffee. "She's at home, Max. She left me."

"Just because you go round blowin' up banks? Can't see why she wouldn't want to be a part of that."

Madison handed him a cup and smiled a bit sadly as she sat next to him on the bed. "I knew you'd be all sympathy for me, old man," she said, knowing that Max wouldn't be Max if he didn't say what was on his mind, and let the rest of the world go hang if it didn't like his opinion. In truth he was a sensitive fellow, but his rugged, unpolished manner sometimes disguised that fact. "Let's get to why you're here. You didn't come to Frankfurt just to find me, did you? Really, Max, you must find a way to get past this male need of yours to come to the rescue."

Max took a sip of the coffee and wiped his mustache with the back of his hand. "I was here before you got here, and for the same reasons, I'm afraid. I think we have a serious conflict of interest . . . Madison, old girl, I'm working with Providence. That wouldn't happen to be your reason for being here, would it now?"

The smile dropped off Madison's face. "Oh my

God." She lowered her coffee cup. "You've got to get out of there. Get on a plane and go back to your farm in Switzerland. Providence is going to fall hard, Max, and I don't want you involved."

"So it is Providence you're after, eh? Workin' for the Yanks again?"

Madison reached for his hand and held it as she spoke. "You told me when you left the IRA that you were finished." She stood up, puffed out her chest and did her best Max Rudger. "Madi, there's no honor in the fight anymore. Just killin' and killin' and there's nothing noble about that. Those were your words, old man, not mine. What happened?"

"An associate in Ireland put them on to me. You know the groups these days, all hooked up to each other. Anyway, they needed an explosives man. There was big money in the offerin'. Enough so I wouldn't have to worry bout nothin'. Anyway, I rolled it round in my head a bit. I thought, I'm fifty somethin', I'm ready to settle down, and I need some security. Then blast if Mossad didn't send a Joe out to talk to me right there in my little Swiss gun shop. They got wind of it somehow and offered me just as much to go in undercover and just tip them off now and then when I heard about an operation planned for Israeli soil. I've done it once too, without exposin' myself. They're happy, I'm happy and Providence is happy cause they got their explosives man."

Madison sat down beside him. "And how many lives have your bombs taken? As many as you've saved?"

"Don't give me that disapprovin' tone of yours, Madi McGuire. You know blasted well that if I wasn't makin' the bombs someone else would be. Besides, the arrangement is only temporary till they can find someone permanent. In a few weeks I'm goin' back to Switzerland, I'm sellin' my place, I'm gettin' married and me and my lovely bride are goin' to live in the prettiest country on God's green earth, Ireland."

Madison's smile had returned. "Max Rudger getting married? I can hardly believe it." She threw her arms around his neck and looked into his bright blue eyes. "Well, congratulations. That's why I haven't heard from you in months. Been busy falling in love, eh? Who is she?"

Max smiled devilishly. "Her name is Helen, born in Switzerland, but I can forgive her that since she wants to live in Ireland with me. She's round and happy and has the prettiest eyes you've ever seen. And she thinks I was sent to her straight from heaven above."

"I'm so happy for you, Max, and for her too. She's a lucky woman."

"It could have been you, Madi, but you never gave me half a chance. Not your type, you said, too much hair." They both laughed at that. "Gettin' back to the business at hand, Mossad knows the CIA was sendin' someone in. They're worried you'll get in my way."

"I don't see any reason why we can't help each other, exchange information and all that. Tell them I won't be a problem. How about Providence? Do they suspect anything is amiss?"

"They don't know what the hell you are. Karl Speigel, Tahril's right hand man, flew to Libya to try and find out somethin' from Libyan Intelligence."

Good, Madison thought, they've already started the background checks.

Max looked at her, a puzzled expression on his face, his blue eyes searching. "Why, Madi? You don't need the money. You've got more Swiss accounts than I have socks. You've never even touched your inheritance, and Lord knows how much you put back all those years. I know how you spook types operate. They give you a few thousand here and there and whatever is left gets put aside cause no one in your government wants anything to do with secret funds. Why come back now?"

"They needed me. And frankly, Max, I need to work. This is what I do. You're probably the only person in the world who understands why I can't walk away. My investment is just too great. It's been my life."

Max Rudger let out a long sigh. "I understand that you, my dear, are deeply disturbed. If I wasn't fifty years old and damn near broke, you can bet you wouldn't find me hangin' round here. Don't you want a normal life? What about Terry?"

"I miss her very much. But I'm not right for her. She wants someone she can shape and mold into her idea of the model partner. I'm not that flexible," she added with a hint of bitterness.

Max patted her knee and shook his head. "You and me, Madi, we're cut from the same mold, we are."

Madison smiled. "You're a dear sweet man, Max Rudger. Now how do you propose we devise a way for your friends to find me."

"Well that's simple enough. I'll just let it slip that you're at the Frankfurter Hof. It's goin' to be a

pleasure to work with you again, old girl. A real
pleasure."

* * * * *

It was well into evening when Max Rudger
returned to Providence headquarters, humming
lightheartedly to himself. He found Karl Speigel and
Michael Peelor talking in one of the back rooms of
the small flat. "Good evenin', gentlemen. Thought I'd
stop by before goin' to my room and see how your
trip went."

Speigel looked up. "Got the scoop on your friend
Madison. Seems she's clean, or I should say, free of
the CIA. We'd like to find her, have a little chat
with her. Don't suppose you know where she's
hiding."

Max filled his pipe and took a pack of matches
from his pocket. He lit the pipe and tossed the
matches on the table. "Don't know that I'd tell you,
Karl, if I did. You're a nasty little bloke sometimes."

Speigel lunged at him, grabbing his jacket. "You
arrogant bastard. You'll do what you're told."

Max looked down at Karl Speigel, who was a
good five inches shorter, and slowly removed
Speigel's hands from his suit. "I could break you in
half with my one hand, you little pecker," he said,
holding Speigel's wrist, his pipe clenched in his
teeth. "Let's get this straight right now. I don't work
for you. I'm here on a commission basis, and as long
as I put the work out you have nothin' to say about
it. You fuck with me, old son, and I'll remove your
testicles." He released Speigel's wrist and looked at

Michael Peelor pleasantly. "Good night, Michael. See you tomorrow."

"Good night, Max," Peelor responded, unable to suppress a grin.

Karl Speigel stood there as the door closed, his face flushed with anger, veins bulging from his forehead.

Peelor looked at him and laughed. "Jesus, calm down, Karl. You asked for it. You've been riding his ass ever since he got here." Peelor reached for the pack of matches Max had tossed on the table, lit a cigarette and then studied the match pack. "Well, look at this. Max Rudger's been at the Frankfurter Hof. That's why he was wearing a suit. Doesn't seem like the kind of place where old Max would hang out, does it?"

Speigel snatched the matches from Peelor's hand. They looked at each other, both having the same thought. "That's it," Speigel yelled excitedly. "I'd bet next month's pay on it. Scorpion is at the Frankfurter Hof. And look at this, the old fart wrote the room number on here."

CHAPTER EIGHT

Terry Woodall sat behind the desk in her office. Not only had she neglected weeks of paperwork, but she had also badly neglected her clients, all three of them. She sighed and absently looked at the television, unable to concentrate. Headline News was on, which had become a habit with her since living with Madison, who seemed to need hourly news updates, and kept the Cable News Network playing nearly all the time. She took a drink of her diet soda and stared at the screen, letting her thoughts stray, not realizing for several seconds what she was looking at. Then she lurched forward, slamming the drink down on the desk.

"Champion or villain?" the anchorwoman was saying. "That is the question West German authorities are asking today after this incredible footage was taken by a tourist in Frankfurt. The woman responsible for this daring rescue is said to be the same woman responsible for the bombing of the Dresdner Bank in Frankfurt."

Terry rushed to the screen as CNN began to show the video tape. Her jaw went slack, she watched in pure astonishment. The hair was different, the woman on the screen wore glasses, but the smooth, fluid movements were Madison's, the thin frame, the unflinching, and sometimes infuriating self-assurance were Madison's. And then, abruptly the footage ended with the automobile exploding, the camera shaking and taking a quick shot of the sky. Terry sat back on her desk and whispered, "Oh my God."

* * * * *

At eight-thirty the following morning, Madison left the hotel and flagged a taxi. The driver, informed that there was a chance she was being followed, weaved in and out of traffic, taking back alleys and side streets until Madison felt sure there was no one behind them. The taxi dropped her near the airport, and she walked another block before stopping at a call box.

After going through the identification procedures, she told the voice on the other end, "The target has made contact. A meeting is scheduled for eight p.m.

this evening at the tavern nearest the Sachsenhauser Warte."

* * * * *

In Washington, D.C., a group of top counter-terrorist officials convened in the White House situation room. Among them were representatives from the State Department, the Pentagon, the CIA, and the Joint Special Operations Command, an antiterrorist force responsible for mobilizing U.S. commandos and coordinating the flow of tactical information to the Joint Chiefs of Staff.

It had been three-ten a.m. in Washington when the Director of Central Intelligence received the first reports that Providence operatives had made contact and arranged a meeting with his agent in Frankfurt. Colby had immediately contacted James Jefferies, the Secretary of State, who in turn contacted the other agencies involved in Operation White Flag.

Now, barely three hours later, they sat at a conference table drinking coffee from Styrofoam cups, a map of Frankfurt on a wall in front of them.

General Harold Granger of the Pentagon, a large man with thick grey hair and a pot belly, smiled with satisfaction. "The bastards bought it, by God. We're almost home, gentlemen." He slapped the table with the palm of his hand. "No one blows up a plane full of Americans and gets away with it."

Jefferies smiled. "Almost only counts with hand grenades, Harry. We've got a long way to go yet." The Secretary turned to Vice Admiral Arthur Koch, commander of the Joint Special Operations

Command. "Arthur, what can you tell us about the meeting place? Can we put it under surveillance without tipping them off?"

Vice Admiral Arthur Koch, a short, stocky, broad-shouldered man with hair too dark for his age, cleared his throat and spoke with a distinct New York accent. "The meeting is in the old section of Frankfurt known as Sachsenhausen, near the Sachsenhauser Warte, which is an ancient watchtower. What could be better for surveillance purposes than a watchtower? In fact, the whole area is perfect. It's crowded with tourists and locals, especially at eight in the evening. I'm confident you could put an asset in the area without being spotted in order to confirm contact."

"Shit, Arthur," General Granger spat, "we want to do more than confirm contact. We want to locate Tahril and blow the sonovabitch away. If we're sure the agent is meeting with Tahril, why not follow them and strike while the iron's hot?"

"I'm afraid that's impossible, General," Arthur Koch answered. "We have Delta Forces on alert and ready to leave the country, but we can't mobilize and formulate any kind of coherent plan of attack in the next few hours. We need more time."

"Delta? Goddamn, Arthur, who said anything about Delta? All we need is one sniper to do the job," Granger stated in his loud, over-confident voice.

Mitchell Colby broke in for the first time. "And risk losing my agent, and a chance to hit the training camps? No way, General. There's no reason for us to do anything but follow our initial plan. We get an asset inside the camps, and then move in.

The Intelligence we can collect in the meantime will be extremely valuable. We're in now. Let's not get excited and lose our heads."

"I agree," James Jefferies said calmly. "We can't justify going into West Germany and risking any loss of innocent life. The response from our Middle Eastern and Soviet friends is going to be bad enough when we hit the camps in Lebanon. The Soviets already believe we're responsible for Kaski's disappearance. From a diplomatic point of view, with the arms talks going on, the last thing we need is more disapproval from the rest of the world."

"A fucking diplomatic point of view? Who cares about that crap now? God, I hate politics," the General grumbled.

"I care about that crap," the Secretary snapped.

Vice Admiral Koch smiled. "Don't worry, Harry. We've gotten permission from Cyprus to land Special Forces there tonight. I can have them in the Bekaa Valley within an hour of the time we get the go ahead. It's just a waiting game now. Damn, Mitchell, I hope to hell your agent is reliable. This operation is going to cost a bundle."

* * * * *

General Harold Granger left the White House seeing one of the great opportunities of his career. He climbed in his chauffeur-driven sedan and closed the window between him and his driver, picked up the telephone and dialed the Pentagon. "This is General Granger. Get me Lieutenant Colonel Paul West."

Moments later West answered, "Yes, General?"

"Paul, how quickly can you have one of our Task Force men in Frankfurt?"

"Seven, eight hours, maximum. Can you brief me?"

"It's top secret, Paul. No one but us and our man gets the details. I want the best marksman we've got, period. Get him in the office and ready to leave within the hour. I'm on my way."

The General smiled as the military sedan raced over the Potomac. "The sissy bureaucratic bastards will thank me for having another option in place. If they use it, I'm a hero. If they don't, no harm done."

* * * * *

Greg Abbott received the confirmation at two-thirty p.m. Washington time. Some four thousand miles away contact had been made. His operative had been spotted near the watchtower at exactly eight p.m. Frankfurt time, and was intercepted approximately twenty minutes later by a man identified as Karl Speigel, a known Providence operative with ties to the Red Brigade, Direct Action, and Baader-Meinhof. When another individual, as yet unidentified, was seen following Madison and Speigel, surveillance was discontinued. The operatives who had been assigned the surveillance detail assumed the unidentified individual was part of a Providence lookout team and, as ordered, backed off immediately for fear of exposure. Although the agents had not been fully briefed, they were aware that the magnitude of the operation was too great to risk being spotted.

Greg Abbott telephoned the Secretary of State

with his report. "We have photographs of the unidentified male. They're being processed through the CIA's Frankfurt station. We should have an I.D. within the hour, although we're pretty sure he's part of a Providence backup team."

* * * * *

Karl Speigel was pleasant, though he had little to say during the forty-minute drive to one of Frankfurt's wealthy residential areas south of the city. Madison, to her surprise, had neither been searched, held at gunpoint, nor blindfolded, and now the weight of the Sig-Sauer tucked tightly in her shoulder holster added a certain assurance to an otherwise nerve-wracking drive.

She attempted to commit the route they drove to memory, but soon found it impossible. Not only was it dark, but there had been too many quick turns, short streets and back roads. Karl Speigel, Madison noted at once, drove like a professional. He had obviously been trained in offensive and defensive driving, techniques not only a vital part of VIP protection, but necessary for a successful escape after a terrorist strike.

When Madison and Speigel had first made contact near the watchtower, Speigel had escorted Madison to a brown Audi. Once she was in the automobile, Speigel checked the underside for electronic devices, the tires for correct pressure, and the lug nuts for tightness, all of which were precautions routinely followed by experienced drivers. During the drive his eyes constantly moved from the road to the side and rearview mirrors. Only a clever professional could have followed without being seen, and that would have required driving without headlights on the dark back roads.

Speigel made a quick turn onto a quiet, tree-lined street. Majestic homes sat on wooded lots nestled against the hillside. Lights from the city glistened below, and Madison realized that Speigel had driven them in circles for nearly forty minutes. In truth, they were not a full ten minutes from the city.

The house was not the fortress Madison would have expected for the head of one of the most dangerous and successful terrorist groups in the world. There was no gate at the end of the winding driveway. No fence surrounding the estate, which sat only a half mile from the street. Madison looked out the window and then at Karl Speigel. "Nice neighborhood. This Mr. Tahril of yours is obviously well off."

Speigel's wide jaw stretched into a tight smile, his white teeth flashed briefly in the dim light. "Ahmed doesn't live here," he said proudly, as if using Tahril's first name carried with it some high degree of position or rank. "This place is on loan. You're wasting your time if you're trying to figure out where we are. It wouldn't help you."

"I wouldn't think of it," Madison answered as the car approached the house and she got her first look at the four bodyguards waiting at the end of the driveway to greet them. Three men and one woman stood facing the car, Uzis simultaneously lowered to their sides with the realization that the driver was one of their own.

She opened the door and stepped out, nodding pleasantly to the guards. "Lovely evening, isn't it?"

Her comments drew no response. Karl Speigel came around the car and took her arm. She nodded again to the guards, then pulled her arm away from Speigel and walked towards the front steps.

The figure silhouetted in the front door light was immediately recognizable — Katherine Maloane had shown her countless photographs and video tapes on the Florida island. Although she could not yet make out his features, there was little doubt it was Ahmed Tahril. Perhaps five feet, ten inches tall, he wore a beige windbreaker, his hands tucked in the pockets of tan corduroy trousers, one shoulder held slightly higher than the other. His hair was thinning, and nearly all grey. The skin was a dark olive, the body plump, rounded, soft. She felt him watching her as she neared him, sizing her up as if she were some object he was thinking of buying, judging her looks and shape, and perhaps her sexual abilities. He was the kind of man she despised.

His voice was soft and fluid. "Welcome, Madison. Please come in. I hope you will excuse the guards for not being more gracious." He extended his hand. "I am Ahmed Tahril. I would be honored if you would please dine with me this evening."

Madison accepted his hand. It was warm and pudgy and she had to will herself not to cringe. "I'm very curious, Mr. Tahril," she said, as he showed her through the door, "about why you want to see me?"

Tahril looked at Speigel. "Leave us, Karl."

"She has a weapon, Ahmed," Speigel protested. "We did not search her as you asked, but I don't think we should leave you —"

"Of course she has a weapon," Tahril broke in gently. "But she will not use it. Why should she? We have a common goal." He patted Speigel on the back reassuringly. "Leave us. It's all right."

Ahmed Tahril led Madison into a lavish den with high ceilings, heavy red drapes, and thick white carpeting. "Cognac?" he asked, walking to the bar.

"Fine," Madison answered, sitting down on the tapestried couch. Tahril sat beside her and handed her the cognac. She studied him silently for a moment before taking a sip.

"You've accomplished a great deal, Madison, considering what you've had to work with." He reached behind the couch and picked up a black bag, setting it between them. Her breathing stopped momentarily. It was one of the bags issued to her by Greg Abbott. Tahril pulled out a handful of wire, the CO_2 pistol, and a small case filled with gunpowder. "Crude but effective weapons. It must be very frustrating for a professional like yourself to work with such tools." He smiled. "We had to search your room. All your things are here now. Nothing has been disturbed. Your money is also here. We took the liberty of checking you out of the hotel. There are many things I would like to share with you. It could take some time. I hope you will understand."

"You took the liberty of checking me out of my hotel and searching my room?" Madison asked angrily. "No, Mr. Tahril, I'm afraid I don't understand. I would appreciate it very much if you would please get to the point."

"The point is, I think I can be of service to each other. I am a Palestinian, Madison, and our organization is called Providence. Have you heard of us?"

Madison nodded. "Of course."

"You have a talent that I am always interested in employing, and I have technology, contacts and a great deal of money available to me. The fact that you are a former CIA agent who has become disillusioned by the unfairness of American policies adds credibility to our cause."

"This is personal, Mr. Tahril. It has nothing to do with Middle Eastern policy, however fair or unfair it may be. I have no interest in lending credibility to your cause." She set her empty glass on the table and stood, looking at Tahril, her green eyes bright, alert. "Now, if you don't mind, I would appreciate it very much if you would return my luggage and have someone drive me into the city."

Tahril, ignoring her request, leaned back on the couch, crossing his legs. "There once was a young girl of twenty-two who joined American Intelligence because she believed America was a great country. She gave the next eighteen years of her life for that country. She fought and killed for that country, as her father fought and killed for that country. And do you know what her country gave her in return? Betrayal and deceit. We have all been betrayed and deceived, Madison. We have been abandoned just as you were abandoned. We share the same pain."

Madison sank back into the couch, and spoke the words she had rehearsed in her mind again and again. "I was blind and very foolish."

Tahril touched her hand gently. "Not foolish, my dear, just very passionate. I can give you an outlet for that passion, an arena for your anger that will force the world to acknowledge the wrongs that have been done. We are small by comparison, but we are light on our feet where the American government is a great, lumbering giant burdened by a lethargic bureaucracy. We can and will succeed. All I ask is that you listen to what I have to say."

* * * * *

Across the Atlantic at CIA headquarters, Mitchell Colby leaned forward and looked at the computer printout that had just been placed on his desk. His eyes hardened, his face turned pale ash. His words were barely discernible as he looked up at the secretary who had delivered the report. "Get me the Secretary of State."

After not quite a full minute he spoke into the phone. "Jefferies, what the hell is going on? Who authorized this? I thought it was understood that I was to approve any action relating to White Flag."

"Good lord, Mitchell, calm down. Of course you have final approval."

"We have a hell of a problem then. Not only has the operation been jeopardized, but the life of my agent is in question at this moment. I want to get to the bottom of this right now."

"Okay, slow down. What's happened?" the Secretary asked, his composed voice not betraying the panic he felt.

"I just got the identification on the man tailing our operative and Karl Speigel in Frankfurt. He's not a Providence operative, James, he's a goddamn Task Force soldier. A government hit man. Worse than that, he's a maverick, we've used him only in special situations. He's a deadly killer and he interprets orders his own way. James, he'll take out Tahril as soon as he gets a chance."

"Oh, Jesus," Jefferies mumbled.

"Abbott wouldn't have done something like this, would he? He's an ambitious little prick."

"No. Greg doesn't have the authority. Besides he's too level-headed. He knows the importance of this operation." There was silence for several seconds, the Secretary's mind churning rapidly, searching for some reasonable explanation. And then it hit him full force. "Granger," he whispered. "General Granger. The Pentagon . . ."

"I'll call you back," Mitchell Colby answered, and then yelled to his assistant, "Get me a secure line to the President, right away, and a driver ready to take me to the Pentagon."

* * * * *

With supper finished, Madison and Ahmed Tahril moved to the terrace and sat down, the cognac in their hands taking the edge off the cool night air.

Tahril was speaking, his voice quiet, somber. "I was fifteen years old when they took Palestine away from us. When my father refused to acknowledge the Jewish State or leave the country for an Arab State, we were moved to the camps where I lived until I was eighteen. Our home and possessions in Tel Aviv were bulldozed. We lost everything. We were treated like animals in a place that had been our ancestral home for two thousand years. The Jews didn't understand why we wouldn't leave. There are so many Arab states, they told us, why not go somewhere else? They never understood that the Palestinian people wanted a homeland too. We wanted back what they took from us. Is that so

110

hard to understand? How could a group of people who had their very existence threatened be so intolerant? The oppressed became the oppressors. Now we are called terrorist and they are called justice."

Madison looked at the man next to her who spoke of oppression and intolerance with such concern, and reminded herself that this was the same man who had ordered the killings of hundreds of innocent people. "It's a very complicated issue. I'm sure any Israeli would present as convincing an argument. You've both been terrorized, you've both been hurt."

The softness left Tahril's eyes, his stare fixed on Madison. "The Israelis are wrong. *That* is the difference. You cannot see this? Israelis have rights. Israelis can vote. Israelis have a voice. Israeli children are not born to live and die in the filth and sweat of the camps."

"Perhaps. But Israeli children die in your war just as painfully as Palestinian children die. Their loved ones mourn just as yours mourn . . . Ahmed, I haven't lived what you've lived. Please don't expect me to share your anger. I told you before, my battle is personal, not political."

Madison took a sip of the cognac, and as she set her glass down she saw a flash. A light reflecting off a metallic object in the darkness below the terrace. Then the tiny red beam from an infrared scope crossed Tahril's forehead. She reacted instinctively, without thought, leaping at Ahmed Tahril, knocking him over in his chair.

At the same moment, the crack of a rifle filled the air, the glass door behind them shattered.

Madison drew her 9mm and moved to the edge of the terrace wall.

Bullets sprayed the terrace wall and dug into the house. The killer in the darkness had switched the rifle to automatic. Madison ducked, using the wall as a shield, then rose and caught a quick glimpse of the light bouncing off the rifle. She fired twice at the reflection, then ducked behind the short concrete terrace wall and waited.

There was silence. Then came the pounding footsteps of Tahril's guards racing through the house. Madison moved to Tahril who was lying flat on his stomach, arms covering his head. "I think it's over. Are you hurt?"

Karl Speigel, flanked by four others burst onto the terrace, their weapons pointed at Madison.

"Lower your weapons," Tahril ordered, breathing heavily. "She saved my life. Get down the hill and find who did this."

He started to get up but Madison touched his shoulder. "Not yet. Stay down till we get a grip on the situation."

Tahril leaned back against the terrace wall and grinned, wiping the sweat from his forehead. "You are very fast, Madison McGuire. I need someone like you."

"And you, Ahmed Tahril, are a born salesman," she answered, looking over the wall, gripping the pistol tightly.

* * * * *

Flanked by a detail of Marines, the Director of Central Intelligence raced down the halls of the

Pentagon, his face red with rage, his blood pressure dangerously high.

"Halt," a uniformed soldier commanded as Mitchell Colby turned the corner on the way to General Harold Granger's office.

"I'm the DCI, Lieutenant," Colby roared without stopping. "I'd advise you to stay the *hell* out of my way."

He swung open the door to Granger's plush office and walked directly to the General, lifting him by his shirt collar, a feat that might have been difficult for even a young man. "You son of a bitch. You're finished."

The General pushed Colby away and straightened his uniform. "What the hell are you doing, Mitchell? Have you lost your mind?"

"You pig-headed bastard. I hope to hell you're happy. You've probably compromised my agent by turning your hired killer loose in Frankfurt," Colby spat with contempt.

"That man is on standby, Mitchell. His orders are to watch and wait. He's there in case we need him, and only if we need him." The General was beginning to perspire. "He's a soldier. He'll follow orders."

Colby looked at him in disbelief. "I don't suppose you bothered to pull the bastard's file. He's a fucking psycho, General, unstable and dangerous and only activated in the most extreme cases. This guy doesn't understand orders. He understands killing."

General Harold Granger lowered himself slowly into his chair. "Oh, Christ," he answered quietly.

"You know, it's dick-heads like you that embarrass us all. And now, General, by way of

Presidential order, I have the distinct pleasure of telling you that you are officially suspended from your duties here and out of Operation White Flag."

* * * * *

Two guards carried the body into the house and laid it on the carpet. "He's dead," Speigel announced, looking at the bullet wounds in the chest and stomach.

"Search him," Tahril ordered.

"Nothing. No papers at all," Speigel reported, after going through the pockets of the camouflage pants and shirt.

Madison squatted to look at the body. She recognized the camouflage tiger stripes as the same type favored by the Special Forces units in Vietnam. She had seen this type of soldier many times and she knew that pride demanded they wear some sort of identifying mark, even though they were not allowed to carry identification. On a hunch she ripped open his shirt. Just as she suspected, tattooed on his chest was a small skull wearing a black beret, a tiny American eagle just above it. Under the logo were the words, *We Kill For Peace.*

Madison sat on the floor, paralyzed by what she had seen. She looked up at Tahril. "He was part of the American Special Forces, probably Task Force One-Sixty. It's an elite group like the Seal Teams or the Rangers. They must have been watching me when I met Karl at the watchtower."

"And I am sure we were both marked for execution," Tahril answered.

"Yes," Madison responded, realizing that the part

she had acted out for Tahril, the portrayal of the betrayed and bitter agent had suddenly become a self-fulfilling prophesy.

How can it be?'

Tahril touched her shoulder. "I would like you to be my guest for a few days and get to know some of my people and our operations. I will contact you very soon to see if you have arrived at a decision. Tomorrow someone will pick you up and take you to our headquarters in the city. You may simply want to act as a bystander, or you may wish to contribute to our operational plans. The decision is yours for now. Is this satisfactory?"

Madison nodded vaguely through the murky vapor that had seized her, still trying to grasp the meaning of these latest events, hearing Terry's words: *They'll use you and then they'll get rid of you. You're expendable.*

"Good," Tahril answered, and then turned to his top operative. "Karl, please explain to me how this man followed you here tonight."

Speigel glanced at Madison, the resentment evident in his eyes. "I don't know, Ahmed. Perhaps you should ask the woman. You would not allow us to search her. She is probably wearing a tracking device."

Tahril laughed, but there was no laughter in his eyes. "She wears a tracking device so that she can kill the man she has led here? Come now, Karl, let us be practical. Were you paid to allow yourself to be followed, or were you simply negligent in your duties?"

Speigel was near panic now. "Neither, Ahmed. I swear it. I was careful. I took precautions."

Ahmed Tahril looked at him in disgust, then leaned forward and pulled Speigel's pistol from his belt. He studied the weapon momentarily, then pointed it at Speigel and pulled the trigger. Karl Speigel dropped to the floor next to the dead American.

Tahril looked at the others, who stared wide-eyed at Speigel's body. "Let this be a lesson to you all. I have no use for ineffective or treacherous operatives. Please dispose of this traitor's body. As for the American's body, we can make use of it."

CHAPTER NINE

It was nearly eleven o'clock that night when Greg Abbott left his State Department office and walked slowly to his automobile, defeated. It had been a disastrous day. A ghastly mistake made by a General so intoxicated by his own power that he had acted alone, without approval, had botched an operation months in the planning. And even more horrible was the probability that Madison McGuire, if she was still alive, had been exposed and could be experiencing interrogation, even torture at this very minute, certain only that she had been deceived.

Abbott climbed into his car and let his head fall back onto the headrest. He had never lost an operative, not this way. Not because of some idiotic error, perpetrated by an official whose only interest was enhancing his career. He clenched his teeth and tried to hold back tears of frustration. But he could not. Alone in his car, Greg Abbott cried aloud for the first time in years.

At length he picked up his cellular phone. "Katherine, I need to see you," he said, his voice shaky, irresolute.

Katherine Maloane flushed at hearing the tone in his voice. They know, she thought in panic; I've been exposed. "What is it?"

"It's Madison. Can I come over? I have to talk to someone."

Katherine smiled. "Sure, I'll be here."

They sat on her sofa, a lone lamp burning on the end table, muted voices from an all news radio station in the background. Katherine Maloane stared at Greg Abbott as he quietly finished his story.

"I told her we'd do everything to protect her," he said. "I promised it wouldn't be like the last operation . . . Damn it, this is my fault. I used all my persuasive powers to recruit her for this assignment."

"I can't believe it. I really can't think of anything happening to Madison. I mean I think Madison could handle whatever happens. God, I really like her, you know?"

Greg Abbott nodded. "I know. It was written all over your face while we were on the island. There was a closeness between the two of you. That's the

118

way I read it, anyway. That's why I knew I could talk to you. I needed to talk to someone who's got some interest in Madison outside the operation, someone with some feelings. Colby and Jefferies and the others, it's just business to them. Maybe I don't have what it takes for this job after all."

Katherine Maloane reached in her purse and pulled out a crudely rolled cigarette. "I got this from a neighbor before you got here. I figured we could use it."

Abbott looked at her and shook his head. "I haven't smoked grass since I was in college. I think I'll pass." He walked to the kitchen. "Got any club soda?"

"Just water. Sorry," Katherine answered, and then suddenly thrust herself off the sofa, hurriedly reaching for the volume on the stereo system.

He ran from the kitchen and they both stood in front of the radio, stupefied, staring blankly at the thing as if looking at it could somehow help them absorb the information.

"After finding the body of an unidentified man on their own front steps, a Frankfurt, Germany news agency reports another bizarre twist in the story of the disgruntled CIA agent who claimed responsibility for the bombings that killed the chairman of the Dresdner Bank," the hollow voice reported. "One hour after the discovery of the body, someone claiming to be a representative of the Providence Liberation Army of Palestine phoned the agency to profess credit for the slaying, saying only that the man was an American and the killing was carried out in cooperation with the former CIA agent, who has apparently joined forces with the P.L.A.P. The

Director of Central Intelligence was not available for comment at this time."

Greg Abbott had reached the telephone before the report concluded.

* * * * *

Ahmed Tahril and Abu Khaled stood looking out the window of Tahril's safe house in Ireland, watching the approaching storm. Purple-black clouds hung ominously and the wind whipped the water into a frothy white lather, slamming it furiously against the rocks below.

"Just look at it, Ahmed. The sheer fury of it is magnificent."

Ahmed Tahril smiled and wrapped his arm around Khaled's shoulders. "It is nothing compared to the storm about to hit America, my friend. More Palestinian lives will be lost, but this time the Americans will be forced to acknowledge the dedication and commitment of our people. We will be the first to penetrate their borders, Abu. We will strike them in their own back yards. They will no longer be able to insulate their people from the truth."

Abu Khaled looked at his leader, his onyx eyes glistening. "Let me go, Ahmed. Let me be a part of this new endeavor."

"No. I need you here to train our young people. They will die for us. We need you alive."

* * * * *

A young man of Middle Eastern descent boarded a plane from Beirut, Lebanon, to Charles de Gaulle airport in Paris. His French was impeccable, his English passable. Dressed in executive clothing, he calmly turned over his briefcase to the French officials for inspection. He had nothing to hide. From Paris he flew to Madrid, Spain, where he was met by an associate and given a new passport. From Madrid he flew four thousand miles to Atlanta, Georgia. At Hartsfield International airport in Atlanta, the young man hired a taxi to take him to an apartment which had been rented for him by an Arab student studying at the University of Georgia. Suffering from severe jet lag, the young man went straight to bed. He knew he must be rested in order to carry out his assignment and avoid being apprehended.

* * * * *

At the same hour, across the Atlantic ocean, a young Middle Eastern woman of nineteen prepared for her first assignment. Like the young man before her, she would first take a complicated route through the capitals of Europe, changing identification at each stop until the U.S. officials could not possibly trace her origin. Light-skinned and educated in England, she spoke English with a distinct British accent. No questions would be asked, no alarms would go out, and no one would know that she had been an operative for the Providence Liberation Army of Palestine since she was seventeen years old.

* * * * *

Greg Abbott, Marge Price, Mitchell Colby, James Jefferies and Vice Admiral Arthur Koch gathered in the conference room adjoining the Director's office on the seventh floor of CIA headquarters. It was barely five a.m. and the coffee pot in the corner of the room had already been emptied and refilled once.

Deputy Director Fred Nolan hurried into the room and laid a single computer printout in front of Mitchell Colby. Colby momentarily studied the paper and then shared its contents with the others. "It's confirmed. The man delivered to the Frankfurt news agency was indeed the same man General Granger ordered to Frankfurt. The most interesting thing is, this man was killed with a Sig-Sauer 226 9 mm handgun. The same type of handgun we issued to Madison McGuire when she first arrived in Frankfurt. I'm not sure I know what to make of it."

"She must be alive," Greg Abbott exulted. "If they'd killed her they'd have delivered her body to the newspaper as well. And if her gun killed that man there's a chance her cover hasn't even been blown."

"Not necessarily," Arthur Koch argued in a somber voice. "They could be waiting for a more opportune time to drop her body somewhere. Or they could be holding her hostage, interrogating her, who knows? They might have used her gun to kill that soldier in order to send us some kind of message."

Mitchell Colby turned to Marge Price. "What if — say for instance — Madison met Tahril somewhere and then General Granger's sniper shows up and tries to kill him. How would Madison react? Would she have interfered?"

"*React* is the key word here, Mitchell," Marge

Price responded, having a great deal of difficulty giving the purely professional response expected of her, still trying to deal with the fact that Madison was in trouble. "That's one of the problems with career agents. They've been conditioned to react, sometimes without thinking. You also have to consider that Madison would have no way of knowing whether she was a target as well, thus making an automatic response even more likely. Knowing Madison, and having worked with career operatives like her, my guess is she would have responded defensively to any outside threat."

"So she may still be alive," Colby said. "And she may have unwittingly rooted herself deeper inside Providence."

Marge nodded. "Given that scenario, yes. It would also explain the reports from Frankfurt. Still, you have to consider the possibility that if she is alive, she may believe she's been double-crossed. You've all seen her file. You know it wasn't that long ago that she *was* set up by a member of our own team. I honestly don't know how she might respond to that possibility. If she is alive, and I hope to God she is, I would be very concerned about her mental stability at this point."

"Are you suggesting that she would actually cooperate with Tahril or join the group?" Jefferies asked.

"Madison McGuire is no terrorist, Mr. Secretary. Quite the opposite in fact. She went out there because she believed in what we were doing. My concern is that she may be more likely to attempt the operation alone, with very little regard to her own physical well-being. On a personal level, she

123

forfeited a great deal to take part in White Flag. She may think she has nothing to lose at this point." Marge paused and studied each face at the table. "Of course, gentlemen, this is all purely speculation and based on the scenario set up by the Director earlier."

Mitchell Colby massaged his temples. The others were silent, each absorbed in his or her own thoughts, each having individual priorities where the operation was concerned.

After several anxious moments, Greg Abbott, who rarely participated in top level meetings, spoke with more authority than he felt. "We have to act on the assumption that Madison is alive and operating under deep cover. There is no real evidence to suggest anything else at this point. Our first priority should be to try and make contact with her. Maybe through the newspapers."

"No way," said Koch, who seemed intent on shooting down Abbott's suggestions. "If she is alive, we'll blow it trying to find her. Shit, Frankfurt is full of spooks who meticulously examine newspapers every day. It's too risky."

"No. Abbott's right, Admiral," the Director announced, looking up from the table. "We can use the media. The bastards have been demanding a statement for days. It's about time we gave them one. I'll clear it with the President today."

* * * * *

Yael Chazan unlocked the door to Providence headquarters, and waited for Madison to pass before following. All activity inside stopped when Madison

124

entered the room and then began again just as quickly. She recognized a man and a woman as two of the bodyguards she had seen the night before. The two were gathering a wide array of weapons, AK-47's, Uzi's and hand grenades, wrapping them in paper and carefully placing them inside large canvas sacks.

A good-looking man with blond shoulder-length hair and a day's worth of beard smiled when he saw her. "You must be Madison," he said with an American accent. "I'm Michael Peelor. Welcome aboard."

Madison knew his name, had seen his file at some point in her career, and her perfect memory recalled the details immediately: a hired gun with a death wish, an unfortunate casualty of Operation Rice Bowl, a rogue wanted by the American Government.

"I'm not exactly on board yet," she said pleasantly. "Still testing the waters."

"The cautious type, huh? You'll have to excuse the mess," he said, pointing to the half-opened desk drawers and mounds of shredded paper on the floor. "It seems we're going to have to relocate."

"What's going on?" Chazan asked, stepping into the chaos.

"We got a tip this morning we'll be raided. Ahmed says we have to move right away," Peelor answered as he fed another stack of paper through the shredder.

"What about the computers?"

"We're leaving everything. I've already wiped out the memories. How about slipping on a pair of plastic gloves and start wiping the place clean?" He looked at Madison. "Sorry, I know this isn't much of a reception for the woman who saved the life of our fearless leader."

Yael Chazan turned to Peelor, face rigid. "You show Ahmed very little respect, Michael. Some of us believe in what we are doing."

"Jesus, Yael, you have no sense of humor," Peelor countered, shaking his head.

Max Rudger stepped out of a back room. "Ah, harmony as usual. That's what I like about this organization . . . Well, hello, Madi, you're a sight for sore eyes." He held out his long arms to her.

"We've really got to stop meeting this way," she whispered as she hugged him.

He winked as he pulled away. "I'm just glad we're on the same side. Heard you were really somethin' last night. Heard the big guy offed our friend Karl too. Can't say I'm sorry to see him go. The little rat."

Michael Peelor laughed. "Max hated Karl, and believe me he wasn't alone." Peelor began distributing airline tickets to Max, Madison and Yael Chazan. "Well, I hate to break up this touching reunion but we have business."

Madison looked at the ticket. Beirut, she thought grimly, an operational nightmare and one of the most dangerous cities in the world for a stranger, a Westerner, and a woman.

Peelor grinned as if he had read her thoughts. "That's right, we're going to Lebanon, where every day is the Fourth of July. Ahmed would like you to join us, Madison. He wants you to get a feel for our operations, maybe even go along on a few. Your safety is guaranteed. We can get you in and out of the country with no problems."

"Hell, you might as well," Max said, tossing the morning paper in her direction. "He's already managed to make the most out of your even considering the possibility."

Madison took the paper and sat down. Moments later she said, "Yes indeed. He's very clever, isn't he? It seems the disgruntled former CIA agent has now joined forces with the radical Palestinian terrorist group. Well, it appears I'm doing a bit more than testing the water, doesn't it?"

Peelor laughed. "Don't worry. You're not committed. Tahril just uses whatever ammo he can find to tick off the U.S. But you might as well go along for the ride. We leave tonight, by the way. Yael and Max leave in the morning. If anyone asks, we're staff members at Beirut University College. There shouldn't be any complications. So, my fellow educators, let's get busy. We have a lot to do in the next couple of hours."

Max wrapped his arm around Madison's shoulder. "Come on in the back and talk to me while I work."

Madison walked with him to one of the back bedrooms. As soon as they were out of sight of the others, Max spun around and faced her, his blue eyes conveying the urgency he had hidden from the others. "Good Christ, Madi, what in bloody hell is goin' on? What happened last night?" he whispered.

Madison looked up at Max Rudger and silently thanked God for his presence. He was her one link to reality, the anchor that kept her from drifting further into the uncertainty of the last twenty-four hours. She sat down in the one chair in the tiny back room, and drew a deep breath. Max could see that she was near exhaustion, dark shadows curved like half moons under the wide green eyes.

"You already know what happened. Someone tried to kill Tahril. An American, Max. He had a Special Forces insignia tattooed on his chest. They tried to take Tahril knowing that it could have blown my cover."

Max Rudger leaned his big frame against the wall, and twisted up one corner of his mustache with his thumb and index finger, as he so often did when he was deep in thought. Then he knelt beside her and whispered. "If all they wanted was for Ahmed Tahril to assume room temperature then they'd have had you do the job. I don't know much about this operation you've gotten yourself into, but I don't think they'd have gone to the trouble and expense of gettin' you this far if the operation wasn't supposed to succeed. It's not logical, is it now?"

Madison shook her head. "No, it's not logical at all. I'm just so gun-shy. I don't want to be used again. I don't need this shit, Max."

"Wait it out. Somethin' went wrong, Madi, old girl. I'd bet my last dollar on it. One of those bleedin' silly pointy heads in Washington screwed it up. If you think it out you'll know that's what happened."

* * * * *

Mitchell Colby and James Jefferies walked purposefully down one of the red carpeted corridors of the White House towards the Press Room.

The Secretary of State straightened his red tie, and cleared his throat. "Shark-infested waters," he mumbled to Colby as they entered the Press Room.

Mitchell Colby stepped behind the podium; the Secretary stood rigidly to his right, hands locked behind his back. "Good morning," Colby said into the microphone while studying the notes in front of him. He looked up at the reporters gathered there, and began, his deep voice booming through the Press Room.

"I'm speaking to you today in response to allegations that a former CIA field agent has become involved with the P.L.A.P. I can assure you these rumors are nothing more than a ploy by a radical group of terrorists to undermine public confidence in our Intelligence agencies, and the government of the United States. Under no circumstances are any American agents or representatives involved in terrorist activities. Unfortunately I must confirm reports that yet another American life has been lost to these senseless attacks by the P.L.A.P. An American businessman was found shot to death in Frankfurt, Germany. We are working closely in cooperation with the West German officials to gain more information concerning the murder. However, in the interest of national security I cannot give you more information concerning the investigation at this time. The Secretary of State will now make his comments and then we will both be available to take your questions."

James Jefferies stepped in front of the podium, his normally soft face creased and drawn from the strain of all-night meetings and too much coffee. "First let me say that this government is tirelessly engaged in an effort to find and prosecute the terrorists responsible for the series of attacks on innocent American lives. The United States of America will never participate in negotiations with terrorists. We will never give in to terrorist demands or threats, and we will never raise the white flag in surrender."

The press conference continued for another forty minutes while the DCI and the Secretary of State answered the countless questions of the Press. The two left the White House, confident that their message would be reported in time to make the evening papers in Frankfurt, Germany.

CHAPTER TEN

They were an attractive couple, thanks to the
man. Short haired, clean shaven, wearing a blue
suit, no tie and a red sweater, he was blond with
light grey eyes and he smiled as he handed over his
boarding pass and carry-on bag for inspection. Had
any of the airline employees been questioned later
about his appearance or manner, they might have
said that there was an open friendliness about him,
or that he seemed a bit less in a hurry than most
Americans in Frankfurt Main airport.
About the woman they would have remembered

little. If not for her outgoing partner she would have been overlooked altogether, for nothing about her particularly stood out. She passed down the aircraft aisle quietly, politely, a faint secondary image searching for her seat, the conservative, if not dull, tweed skirt brushing inconspicuously below her knees, thick-rimmed glasses surrounding her eyes, obscuring their brilliant green . . . Blending in is what spies do best.

Once the couple was comfortably in the air, the freshly shaven Michael Peelor released his seat belt and leaned back in his chair, taking out a newspaper. Seconds later he let out a slight chuckle and gently elbowed Madison.

"Listen to this. That old fart Colby at the CIA says they've never heard of you. They deny you were ever associated with them. Oh, and get this, the Secretary swears dramatically that America will never raise the white flag and surrender to terrorists' demands. Strong stuff, huh? He really went out on a political limb there."

Madison smiled. "Such a cliche statement to . . ." Her voice trailed off and Peelor looked up from his paper.

"You okay?"

"Yes. May I see that paper?"

Michael Peelor looked a bit confused as he handed over the newspaper. But he soon refocused his attention on the travel guides in the pocket of the seat before him.

Madison read James Jefferies statement through twice. *We will never raise the white flag.* It *was* a cliche statement, the type used in a political campaign maybe, but not the type used by the

Secretary of State in a serious press conference on terrorism. Slowly she looked up from the paper. Of course, she thought, it's so simple it's beautiful. Max had been right. Something must have gone wrong and now they were trying to tell her. She laid the paper on her lap and leaned her head back on the seat, eyes closed.

* * * * *

Beirut, Lebanon, a city of extreme contrast. Lebanon's cosmopolitan center of culture and commerce, the city once called the Paris of the Middle East. Now a city divided into sections held by Christians and Muslims while the twelve-year-old civil war raged on. A waterfront port with sandy beaches and modern apartment buildings on the west, a war-torn battleground in the southern slums. A city now home for thousands of Palestinian refugees living in camps or slums on the edge of the city. A city that had unwillingly become the home base of some and the target for others in the Arab-Israeli conflict.

And even on a quiet day, the fear that burned in the hearts of the people was as hot as the glaring Mediterranean sun, and the tension was as constant yet as erratic and unpredictable as the roving gangs of men and boys who walked the city streets with their automatic weapons. Beirut, Lebanon, a city on fire.

Michael Peelor looked at Madison as they drove on the east-west road which ran from Beirut east to Damascus, Syria. "I'd take you on a tour of the city but without the right credentials we'd be dead. Roadblocks are all over the place. This area is pretty safe, but you want to be real careful in the rest of the city. Tomorrow we get fresh ID's. The last thing we want to be in Beirut is American or British. The Christian militia runs the east side, the Shi'ite Muslims are to the south, Palestinian Arabs make up about ninety percent of the population, and here, in this section, it's pretty much a mixed bag. Lots of business people, embassy officials and journalists." Peelor looked at himself in the rearview mirror. "I think I'll let my hair grow out again. No point in sticking out."

They turned onto the two-lane seaside road which ran by the Corniche, Beirut's crowded Mediterranean promenade, an area that seemed unaware of the hell that reigned every day in other parts of the city, and headed west past an eight-story hotel with a sign out front that said AMERICAN EMBASSY.

"Just look at it," Peelor told her, shaking his head incredulously. "Sitting there with no wall around it and only two crummy Marine guards at the front door. They've been building the new embassy for years but the civil war nearly halted construction. So they leased this hotel."

Madison took a second look at the big, modern, coral-pink building, then glanced back at the ex-Delta Force commando. Would the embassy be Providence's next target? She sensed something more to Peelor's comments other than merely casual conversation, but she dared not pursue it. He could be testing her, for she knew there was another test coming.

Ahmed Tahril was not the type of man to take anything at face value. He would know that even classified files could be altered to mislead, **and** disinformation could have been fed to his **connections** at Libyan Intelligence. At some point they would **test** her allegiance — of this she was certain. Hinting that the American Embassy was a target could be **a** clever ruse meant to lure her into a trap. If **a** warning was sent out or security around the embassy increased, Providence would be alerted **to** her duplicity. Still, she knew, it was a risk she **must** take.

* * * * *

"Mr. Colby, this is Greg Abbott. It's been **over** twenty-four hours now and still no word from **our** asset. I have an idea, sir, a hunch really, and I **need** your help to follow through."

The Director of Central Intelligence smiled. He liked Greg Abbott. He was young and hungry **and in** many ways he reminded Colby of himself at the **age** of forty. "We've got agents all over Germany **and** we're still not getting any reliable Intelligence. At this point, son, I'd be glad to go with a hunch."

"Thank you, sir. I need a small work space **at** Langley and all the satellite photos of the **terrorists'** camps in Lebanon that you can clear me for. I'd **like** to study them, see if there's any increased **activity.** And I need my calls routed directly to Langley **in** case she tries to make contact."

"You think she's in Lebanon?"

"All I know is that she has disappeared, sir. **She** may already be in the camps."

Mitchell Colby held the receiver in his hand **for a** moment after Abbott was gone, then buzzed **his** assistant. "Get me Vice Admiral Koch at the JCOS, please." Moments later the Vice Admiral was on the line. "Arthur, I'd like to increase our reconnaissance flights over Lebanon."

"Jesus, Mitchell, we've got hostages there somewhere. If those fanatics spot our aircraft they're going to get nervous, and I don't know how safe that would be for our people in captivity. Besides, we have to get permission to increase activity. After all, it's not our air space. We're already making sweeps of the area every few hours and recording every phone call we can going in and out of the city. And our satellites pass a couple times a day. What's the problem?"

"Our missing asset may be there, Arthur. No confirmation yet."

"Good God," the Admiral murmured, barely audible. "We may be closer to putting the operation in motion than we thought."

"Maybe. But then she could be a hostage herself . . . Listen, Arthur, I need to get those surveillance tapes in the hands of my analysts as soon as they're recorded. Not a week or a day later. I need them relayed immediately. We don't have any time to waste."

"I'll have the visuals relayed after every sweep. Keep me up to date, Mitchell. I've got fifty Delta commandos on hold in Cyprus."

* * * * *

The house in which Ahmed Tahril stayed when visiting Beirut, the house which would serve as temporary headquarters for the four operatives who

136

had been forced to leave Frankfurt, was built in traditional Lebanese style with thick limestone walls and an orange tiled roof. But it had been westernized in that it was large, two levels, with a deck surrounding the top level, and it sat in a wealthy Christian area on the edge of the city along the Mediterranean coast.

Michael Peelor led Madison through the house, showed her the kitchen, the living room, the four bedrooms, and then led her through a locked door leading off the kitchen. The room was about the size of a two-car garage, and had probably been just that at one time. But now it was carpeted and painted, and filled with sophisticated office equipment — work stations complete with computers and multi-line telephones. There was a fax machine, a copy machine, and, of course, the indispensable paper shredder.

"So, now you know your way around," Peelor said as they walked back into the kitchen. Then a strange expression crossed his face. It was the first time Madison had seen him remotely serious. He lifted himself up and sat on the kitchen counter. "It's incredible, isn't it?"

"You mean the house? Yes, it is very nice."

"No. I mean it's incredible that Tahril stays here while the Palestinian brothers he claims to love so much live in the camps and the slums. What an asshole."

Madison was surprised by his willingness to criticize the man he worked for, the man he trained young operatives to kill for. Perhaps there was hope for Peelor, she thought, perhaps there was some decency left in him.

"If you feel that way," she said, searching the kitchen cabinets for a glass, "why not leave? Why do something you don't believe it?" She found a glass and filled it with water.

He shrugged. "War is war. In the end it doesn't really matter whose side you were on."

Madison lowered the glass. "Oh, but it does matter, Michael. It's the only thing that matters in this kind of war."

But he did not hear, or perhaps he did not want to hear. His face had lost its seriousness and he was smiling again. "Well, I'm going to get some shuteye," he said brightly, jumping off the counter. "See you in the morning."

* * * * *

Katherine Maloane walked into her State Department office and closed the door behind her. From her purse she removed the envelope, which she had picked up at the cafe less than an hour ago, and stared blankly at its contents. The payment she had expected was not enclosed. Katherine unfolded a neatly typed note and looked at it in horror.

WARNING–BLUEBIRD. FRANKFURT AGENT REPORTS MISINFORMATION PASSED AT PREVIOUS DROP. NO AGENT SCORPION ARRIVED FRANKFURT AM MAIN. RADIO REPORTS OF DEFECTED CIA AGENT ARE AMERICAN SMOKE SCREEN. POSSIBILITY YOU HAVE BEEN DETECTED.

Katherine Maloane had no way of knowing that Yuri Vissarionvich Kaski had filed the false report to

KGB headquarters or that he had decided to deal with Madison McGuire on his own.

She leaned back in her chair, her heart pounding furiously, wondering if she had been found out, wondering if it was possible that the State Department had intentionally fed her misinformation. Although Katherine had never received a direct warning, she was well aware that the KGB dealt very harshly with agents who passed bad Intelligence.

Hands trembling, she stuffed the typed note into her bag and rushed out of her small office, nearly knocking over Greg Abbott on her way down the long corridor, the contents of her bag spilling out on the tiled floor.

Abbott, who was on his way to Langley, briefcase in hand, squatted down to help her clean up the mess. "In a hurry, huh?" Then he looked at her, looked at the pale face, the red eyes. "Are you all right? Are you sick?" he asked, picking up the last item from the floor, the partially folded sheet of paper that Katherine had stuffed into her bag. He saw the word *Bluebird* as he handed it over, but it meant nothing to him.

Katherine snatched the note from him. "Yes. I'm going home."

Abbott watched her hurry down the hall, watched her turn and look back at him before stepping onto the elevator. It was a scene that repeated itself in his mind several times that day, although he was not yet sure why the encounter had disturbed him so.

CHAPTER ELEVEN

Another dawn, another bed, another city. Madison woke to the sound of gunfire in the distance. Or was it a jackhammer, or a truck backfiring? In Beirut one could never be certain. She rolled over in the bed that had been assigned to her and saw the sky beginning to brighten through the cracks in the white shutters of the bedroom. She was alone. Terribly alone. Still she knew that she did her best work when she was alone. Like the poet who cannot create until love had once again escaped her, and so she played it out again and again, loving and losing, sure that one day in her aloneness the masterpiece inside her would seize her pen and guide it over blank pages.

Madison heard water rushing through tired pipes. Heard the bathroom door open, heard Peelor's footsteps going happily down the stairs. She knew he was smiling. He was always smiling. She heard the telephone ring, heard his voice whispering into the receiver. The spy in her wanted to get up, wanted to listen in, but the poet rolled over and closed her eyes.

A knock at the bedroom door. He was going to the airport to pick up Max and Yael, coffee was ready downstairs. Moments later the spy was standing at the window watching the gold Honda with Lebanese plates drive away.

Ten minutes later Madison, showered and dressed, was walking towards the garage door. Peelor had neglected to lock it after their tour of the house last evening, and Madison had spent a good portion of the night struggling with whether to investigate the room while he slept or wait for a more opportune moment.

She tried the file cabinet first. It was locked. She then advanced to one of the computers, flipped the red switch and attempted to gain access to the directory. This she managed, even though her knowledge of computers was limited and she did not understand the logic of the keys she pressed. She highlighted a coded title with the cursor bar and viewed the file, but it was in Arabic, a language Madison did not speak or read.

Frustrated, she muttered an obscenity and leaned back in the chair, tugging at a desk drawer. It revealed paper clips, a few rubber bands, a chewed pencil, and fingernail clippers. She opened another drawer and smiled. There were papers in this drawer, bound together with rubber bands and separated into three small stacks with a top sheet of paper which listed a name, the time period involved and a dollar amount. Two of the amounts were American dollars, one Lebanese pounds.

Madison removed the band from a stack and turned the top sheet over. Slowly she began to understand what she was looking at. The possibility that terrorist operatives were required to mail in regular expense reports had never occurred to her, yet this was apparently what she had found. Providence was more of a business than a cause, and that, in and of itself, was a frightening realization. It crossed her mind that pure luck had led her to find these reports now, as it had so many other secret documents and so many other desk drawers in so many other hidden rooms over the years. But then so much of spying was luck and timing, and these particular papers had, no doubt, been destined for the computers and then the shredder, and had merely been left as an oversight by a hurried bookkeeper.

She searched the papers looking for some clue that might help her know Providence's operational plans. There were copies of airline tickets, rental car agreements, restaurant receipts, and the occasional hand-written note listing the cost of some item for which the purchaser had failed to obtain a receipt.

One such note reported that the cost of an AR-15 assault rifle had been two hundred American dollars.

Madison studied the note and then flipped back to the top sheet and looked at the information. Abu Liftawi — March 31 thru April 15 — $6,341.00. She then checked the airline tickets. It was no great surprise to find that Abu Liftawi had flown under an assumed name. The surprise was the last airline ticket. Mr. Liftawi had flown from Madrid, Spain, to Atlanta, Georgia.

Madison instantly became alarmed. She shuffled quickly through the papers committing times, dates, names and locations to memory, not a difficult feat because she was blessed with the gift of total recall.

More than half of the expenses had been incurred in the United States. *Oh Christ, they have operatives in the States.* Although she remained calm and continued her search in an orderly manner, her mind was racing. She started through the second pile of expenses. Galla Attawa — March 31 thru April 15 — $7,736.41. Final destination, New York City.

Madison spun around in the chair and looked at the telephone. It wasn't safe. She would have to find another way. The fax machine, she thought. If she could figure out how to use the fax machine she could send copies of the reports to the American Embassy in Beirut. They would be just as alarmed. They would alert the CIA and the FBI to the fact that terrorist operatives had penetrated U.S. borders. She grabbed all three stacks of papers and headed for the machine. Instructions, where the hell were the operating instructions? She lifted the lid on the machine and peered inside. Nothing. And then voices . . . The front door closing . . . She had lost track of time. How long had she been in this room? Hurriedly she stuffed the papers back in the drawer and switched off the computer.

By the time Michael Peelor, Max Rudger and Yael Chazan walked into the kitchen, Madison was leaning against the counter clutching a cup of coffee in both hands, presenting them all with the most innocent look she could muster.

Max gave her a bright, knowing smile. It had been his big voice that had broken her concentration and gotten her out of the room in time.

* * * * *

The morning crept by. Michael and Yael seemed to be waiting for something. Occasionally Michael would come out of the garage and the two would form a sort of huddle and speak in conspiratorial tones.

Max sat idly on the couch, smoking his pipe, watching one of the three Lebanese television stations, seeming completely oblivious to what was going on around him. He knew that Madison had found something while Michael had left her alone in the house. He had seen it on her face when they had returned from the airport; he had felt the tension she concealed from the others.

Occasionally he glanced at her from his position on the couch. She sat a few feet away at a dining room table nursing a cup of coffee. When Yael approached and informed her that she would be invited to witness a major operation that would further both of their agendas, Madison responded indifferently while she played with a cigarette lighter.

"Forgive me, Yael, if I don't seem overwhelmed. But since I met Ahmed Tahril I've seen nothing to convince me that any of you are capable of carrying out an operation." She looked up slowly from the cigarette lighter and added, "Frankly, I think I was doing rather well on my own. At least I was doing *something.*"

Max smiled to himself. She was challenging the young terrorist, drawing her out, forcing her to give up more information than she had intended. And even though it was obvious that Yael was suspicious of Madison, Yael was not yet in total control of her emotions, a fact that had not been lost on either Max or Madison.

Yael turned to Madison angrily and spat her words. "We *are* doing something. We are waiting for explosives from Damascus. The operation is aimed at the Americans. We want them out of Lebanon, out of the Middle East. How do you feel about that? Because no matter what the others believe about you, I know that in your heart you are still an American."

A strange smile crossed Madison's face and left just as quickly. "It is my American eyes that need convincing," she said, and joined Max on the couch, leaving Yael standing frustrated at the dining room table.

Max smiled stupidly as if he had heard none of what had been said. "I tell you what, love, you haven't seen anythin' until you've seen *Dallas* on Lebanese television. I swear to you, old girl, I

145

thought I would pee my pants when I saw J.R. Ewing speaking Arabic in that cowboy hat."

Madison laughed, and at the same time Yael stormed out. They felt a surge of tension rush from the room. They heard the garage door slam.

"Really got her goin', didn't you?" Max mumbled with a chuckle.

"She's just playing hard to get," Madison said with a smile. She went to the garage door and knocked. "Sorry to disturb you, Michael, but did you get those new ID's ready for us yet? I need to pick up a few things in town. Half my clothes are still in Frankfurt and I'd like to get to the bank and convert some funds. Need some running clothes too. Have to stay in shape, you know."

At the sound of an engine, Max looked out the window. "We've got company," he yelled.

Yael returned to the room. Michael Peelor strode outside and spoke with the driver of a large yellow Mercedes truck while Madison, Max and Yael watched from the window. He returned with the driver beside him, a dark young man who barely looked old enough to drive. He led the boy to the kitchen, and turned him loose. The young man began searching the refrigerator, eating whatever he could find as if he hadn't seen food in days.

Michael came back into the dining room and said to the three of them, "Everything is in place. Max, it's time for you and me to go to work. Yael, you can take Madison to the bank, and then drop her at the Corniche. There are all kinds of Western-type shops around there. Just be sure the two of you are at the cafe by four o'clock sharp. Yael knows which one."

* * * * *

Abu Liftawi sat in the rented Collier Road apartment in Atlanta, Georgia, carefully cleaning the AR-15 fully automatic assault rifle he had purchased for two hundred dollars a few days before. He was excited, but not nervous, knowing he was about to do what he had never done before. He could hear the words his leader had spoken on the day he finished training in the Bekaa Valley camps: "You are our future," Ahmed Tahril had told the group. "You will lead us into battle boldly and bravely."

Liftawi loaded a full magazine clip into the rifle and shoved a .22 caliber pistol in his belt. He slipped on a long raincoat, secured the rifle under one arm, and checked himself in the mirror before walking out. On the way to the car he stopped at the trash bins and tossed in all the copies of airline tickets and false passports he had used to get into the United States. In one of his coat pockets was a note written in Arabic which gave his true name and identified him as a member of the Providence Liberation Army of Palestine. His name, he thought with great pride, was a name that would not be easily forgotten by the end of this day.

* * * * *

With fresh ID's in their pockets, Yael and Madison drove along the two-lane seaside road past the tall modern apartment houses and rocky headlands that line the beaches of Lebanon's capital city. Yael parked the car on a busy street near the Corniche's shops and pavement cafes and informed

147

Madison coolly that whatever she needed was within walking distance. It became painfully clear to Madison that finding time to use a telephone was going to require some very creative measures.

Their first stop was the Bank of Lebanon, one of nearly a hundred banks that operated in Beirut, the city that, before the war and the fall of the Lebanese pound, had been considered the financial capital of the Middle East. The bank seemed undisturbed by the war around it, yet just yards away another building had been bombed and reduced to piles of huge concrete slabs with twisted and gnarled steel reinforcement sticking out the ends. Yael waited near the door inside the bank while Madison spoke French, the second language of the Lebanese people, to a bank clerk. After a brief conversation she was given an astounding twenty-seven hundred Lebanese pounds in return for one thousand Deutsche marks, about five hundred American dollars.

Madison took her time in the small specialty store on the promenade, and picked out two pairs of gym shorts, socks, a pair of sweats and a pair of running shoes.

On the way back to the car to drop off the shopping bags, Madison told Yael, "Never imagined I'd be buying gym shorts in Beirut."

"What did you expect?" Yael asked with the edge in her voice that always seemed to be there when she addressed Madison. "You are surprised that the people are so civilized in this part of the world. That is what you are trying to say, is it not?"

Madison touched her arm as they were crossing the street, and Yael spun around defensively.

"Please," Madison said, "I didn't mean that as an insult. I'm just a bit taken aback by the fact that life goes on in such an ordinary way during a civil war. It really says something for the resiliency of the people here."

"One grows accustomed to living with war. You know that as well as I," Yael said, watching the ground as she walked. "This was a beautiful place once. My family came here when I was a child before the war started in 'seventy-five. Now part of the city has been shelled by the Israelis in an attempt to destroy the headquarters of the Palestinian groups who operate here. And the civil war has part of the city living in the ruins of shelled buildings and apartment houses with broken out windows."

"Where is your family?" Madison asked, reaching for a cigarette and finding an empty pack.

"In Israel. They are Israeli Jews," Yael answered quietly.

"Why are you fighting against your own people?"

Yael stopped and looked at her, the dark brown eyes probing. "Why are you, Madison McGuire?" She did not wait for an answer. She began walking again. Madison thought she had lost her, thought she had pushed too far, but Yael spoke again, quietly at first. "I had a friend who was Palestinian. In nineteen eighty-one his family was driven from Israel. They came here and lived in the refugee camps in the Israeli-occupied part of Western Beirut. My friend watched the Christian militia, flanked by Israeli soldiers, kill hundreds of unarmed Palestinian civilians in a raid on the camps one night. The Israeli soldiers had been ordered by their own

149

government not to intervene, even though it was telling the Israeli people all along that it wanted to promote peace talks with the Palestinians. Rafik's entire family was murdered that night, including his ten-year-old sister. He was smuggled back to Israel where he began organizing groups and encouraging the people in the occupied territory to fight. He was killed in Gaza for attacking an Israeli soldier. Do you know what was his weapon? He had a rock in his hand. They shot him for throwing a rock. I have since denounced any ties I had with the Israelis. They are no longer my people. My heart is with the Palestinians."

"I'm sorry for what you've been through, Yael, for what you've lost," Madison said.

Yael's eyes swept over her suspiciously. "Come, we must meet Michael soon at the cafe."

"But it's only three o'clock," Madison objected. "There's an open air market just ahead. I'll just pick up a few things and meet you at the cafe. Where is it?"

"Back where the car is parked. The Cafe Daniel," Yael answered, unsure, and then grabbed Madison's wrist and held it tightly, her sharp features contorted. "You must be there by fifteen minutes before the hour. Let me warn you now, Madison, if you have plans to betray us, Ahmed will find you and have you killed."

Madison looked at the hand around her wrist and then slowly raised her eyes to Yael's face.

Yael released the wrist almost involuntarily. Madison's eyes had frightened her.

Yael watched Madison walk into the crowded market. She tried to keep an eye on her, but

Madison, wearing jeans like many of the market shoppers, and a dark scarf around her red head, quickly faded into the crowd. Reluctantly, Yael turned and headed towards the cafe.

It was the first opportunity Madison had had to see the old-world side of Beirut, the tiny section typical of every ancient city where hundreds of years of history remained somehow untouched by the modern world. The women behind the fruit stands wore long dresses of bright blue and yellow with ankle-length black pants underneath. The old men stood proudly behind their stands or stalls, haggling with customers in Arabic over the price of a banana, wearing white headdresses and bright handwoven jackets too thick for the hot Mediterranean days. The stalls and stands were jumbled together in different stages of disarray. Baskets of grain and barley cluttered the walkways, and the sweet smell of warm melons and Lebanese coffees filled the air. It was total chaos. Just the type of place where one could easily disappear.

Madison stopped by a small stand and spoke in French to the woman standing there. "Please, can you tell me where there is a telephone?" But the woman did not seem to understand, and Madison, feeling a bit guilty about walking away without making a purchase, ended up buying grapes and bananas and the most beautiful apricots she had ever seen. The woman gave her a basket in which to carry her bundle, and Madison left an extra fifty pounds on her table.

A man wearing a business suit finally answered her question. "The Commodore Hotel. There are may foreigners there. Just around the corner, one block."

Fifty American dollars persuaded the reluctant manager to allow her to use his private line in the back office rather than the public telephone in the lobby. Nearly ten minutes of struggling through the agonizingly slow steps necessary to make an international call left her less than thirty-five minutes to get to the cafe when Greg Abbott's voice came on the line.

Madison smiled. "So what happened, Abbott? Were you betting I could shoot my way out, or was I a target too?"

"Madison? Thank God. Listen to me. Something went haywire in Frankfurt. Someone got their signals crossed. It was a mistake, Madison. No matter what you're thinking, you weren't set up."

"Glad to hear it. Actually I've thought it over, you see, and I came to that conclusion on my own. I saw the message in the paper. Listen, I'm in Beirut and this morning a truck from Damascus pulled into Tahril's driveway. I think it's loaded with explosives. I've been told an operation is planned for today. I'm to meet two Providence operatives, Peelor and Chazan, at a pavement cafe on the promenade by four my time. The promenade is across the street from the American Embassy."

"My God. That's less than a half hour away. We'll warn them right away. But we'll have to figure out a discreet way to evacuate the building without tipping off Providence and blowing your cover."

Mitchell Colby, who had been sitting across from Greg Abbott at Langley, heard Madison's voice over the speaker and was already out of his chair and on another telephone. "Get me our embassy in Beirut, pronto." He covered the mouthpiece and looked at

Abbott. "We've got over two hundred people in that building."

"Providence has people in the States," Madison was telling Abbott hurriedly. "One in Atlanta whose name is Abu Liftawi. He flew from Madrid to Atlanta using the name Marcus Echeverria on April thirteenth. He purchased an AR-15 assault rifle on the fifteenth. There's also a woman using the name Cheryl Kohler who flew into New York City on the fourteenth. Her real name is Galla Attawa. They're planning a strike, but I don't know when or where."

"The Director is sitting right here, Madison. We'll have people on their way to find out in a matter of minutes. And we'll do what we can to alert the Embassy. Tell us what happened. How did you get to Beirut?"

Madison gave him a condensed version of the events in Frankfurt the night the Task Force soldier had been unlucky enough to try and kill Tahril while she was sitting next to him. She told him briefly about Tahril's reaction and his shooting of Karl Speigel, about Providence's Frankfurt headquarters being abandoned after a tip about a raid, and she gave him the address of Tahril's Lebanese residence.

"Madison, are you all right? How are you holding up?"

Madison sighed deeply. "Frankly, I'm scared out of my mind. Right now I'm looking out the window of the Commodore Hotel. I can see a group of men firing on a jeep full of soldiers. The hotel floor is shaking because some part of the city is being shelled, and the only phrase I know in Arabic is, Yes, I will be happy to stand very still with my hands over my head . . . And now I have an appointment to witness some gruesome and no doubt horrifying act of violence. Does that give you an idea of how I'm doing?"

"Hang in there, Madison. We haven't had Intel like this out of the Middle East in years." He paused while Colby handed him a note. "Here's your contact codes and numbers. Radio frequency will be forty point nine-three. Use this information if you get into the camps to relay your location. We can have people there within an hour. Good luck, Madison."

Madison memorized the numbers and codes and left the hotel at three-forty, running with the basket of fruit in her hands.

Yael Chazan was sitting at the pavement cafe, innocently sipping a cup of tea, looking as if she wished no one any harm. Madison slowed her pace, caught her breath and glanced at the embassy across the street. About one hundred Lebanese men and women waited in a line in front of the embassy to apply for visas. The circular drive led off the main road and had no barricade. The building was tall with windows and balconies which would, Madison gauged, make it structurally weak.

She sat down across from Yael. "You see, I merely picked up a few things and came back here like a good little soldier. What's happening. Where's Michael?"

"He will meet us later," Yael answered, abruptly distracted by the sight of the yellow truck that had just passed the cafe. "We must go to the car now."

They were crossing the street, only yards from the automobile when Madison spotted the truck again. It had circled the block and came back around and parked at the end of the street, its engine idling. Madison paused before climbing into the car, looked at the truck then back at the embassy, and suddenly the entire plot became horribly clear.

The boy behind the wheel was going to die, the same young man who had opened the refrigerator earlier in search of what Madison now knew was his last meal.

Then she saw a slow, steady stream of embassy vehicles pulling out from behind the building. The evacuation was slow and ineffective, but at least some of the people were managing to get out.

"Get in," Yael demanded, pushing open the passenger door from the inside.

Madison stared through the front window as Yael drove around the block and parked behind the yellow truck at the end of the street, several hundred yards from the embassy. The driver, seeing that Yael's car was safely behind the truck, raced the engine and slammed the vehicle into gear. It lurched forward with a slight lift of its front end, and roared down the busy street.

Madison looked at the full tables at the Corniche's cafes, looked at the line of Lebanese waiting for their travel documents in a last futile attempt to escape the war in their country, looked at the pedestrians in the streets, and everything inside her — that iron sense of justice, that self-regulated perception of wrong and right, that need to believe in the rightness of the side she had chosen — wanted to cry out. But she felt Yael's dark eyes probing her, felt the desire in young Yael to expose

Madison's duplicity, and she stifled the cry that had lodged itself in her larynx, knowing that she could be no more than a hushed collaborator, a mute accomplice to massacre.

The driver detonated his load at the exact moment of impact. Screams filled the air, and thick brown smoke. The embassy walls broke apart and crumbled to the ground. A traffic light in front of the building curled and melted from the intense heat, dripping to the street like a hot crayon. On the square, tables and chairs had been blown backwards, while their occupants, the ones who had survived the blast, scattered in horror. The roof of a nearby gift shop began to melt and then collapsed on a crowd of people who had made it as far as the doorway.

The rear car door opened and Michael Peelor, who had been watching the operation from elsewhere, climbed in. "Let's go," he ordered.

Yael made a U-turn and screeched away. "It is done," she murmured, glancing at her passenger. "Many are dead. How does it make you feel, Madison McGuire?"

"Casualties are just another part of war." Madison answered, but the quality and tone of her voice were so strange and distant that Yael turned back to her.

Madison locked her gaze on Yael, the green eyes eerily detached like the eyes of a phantom peering through the holes in a phantom's mask. Yael quickly turned away again, unable to endure the strange stare.

* * * * *

A detail of six special agents from the Atlanta division of the FBI piled out of two cars at the Collier Road apartments. Two agents covered the back, two positioned themselves behind open car doors, and two ran to the front of the building. One firm kick administered just below the doorknob by Special Agent Alex Trever sent the door swinging open. The agents quickly made a sweep of the apartment, guns drawn.

"Shit," said Trever. "We're too late."

* * * * *

Abu Liftawi parked the rented Buick along the road next to Piedmont Park, and walked across the street towards the high school. It was time for the morning break, and he could see several students sitting under trees and at picnic benches, see them standing in groups smoking cigarettes, laughing. He hated the sight of them, hated their freedom, hated their laughter, hated them because they were Americans.

He prayed to his god as he walked toward martyrdom, and silently condemned the young Americans who stared at him blankly as he pulled the AR-15 from under his raincoat and opened fire. When one clip was expended and a fresh group of faces came pouring from inside the school to see what was happening, he calmly installed another and fired again. When he was satisfied that he had fulfilled his mission, he withdrew the .22 caliber pistol, placed it against his temple and squeezed the trigger.

In a matter of minutes local radio and television

programs interrupted their programs with bulletins, and horrified parents fled their homes and businesses, terrified that their children were among the thirty-two reported dead at Grady High School.

Local police arrived on the scene within minutes. FBI agents, converging on the schoolyard, insisted that it was a matter for the Federal Bureau of Investigation and not local authorities. Sealing off the scene, they took charge of the body, the weapons and any evidence left behind.

* * * * *

In Washington, D.C., the Directors of the FBI and the CIA, and the head of the Senate Task Force on Terrorism met to discuss the cover-up, for it could not be made public that a terrorist organization had penetrated the borders of the United States. To acknowledge their success, the FBI Director reluctantly agreed, would only satisfy the terrorists' objective of undermining public confidence in America's Intelligence and law enforcement agencies.

The FBI would immediately begin creating a false identity for the terrorist, Abu Liftawi. They would manufacture background information about the man which would be handed to the local law enforcement agency and made available to the media, complete with paid informants who would swear they had worked with the disturbed young man or had known him since he was a child.

* * * * *

At the same moment in New York City, FBI agents searched the apartment of Galla Attawa, the second Palestinian terrorist who had been sent to the United States on a suicide mission. Cuffed, she sat defiantly mute on the sofa while FBI agents wrapped an Uzi submachine gun and nearly a pound of plastic explosives in plastic bags and carried them out of the apartment.

* * * * *

Ahmed Tahril smiled with satisfaction as he watched television from his leather chair in his Ireland safe house. He had just seen the pile of rubble that had once been the American Embassy in Beirut. He listened in fascination to the statements of outrage pouring forth from American government officials. He saw their bloodshot eyes, their grave faces, heard the trembling in their voices as they announced that sixty-three people had been killed. He could not have been more pleased. Yet another state-sponsored operation had been a success. A travel warning had been issued, and all civilians and embassy personnel were required to board military flights at once and leave the country.

It was what he wanted, what all the Arab States wanted. They had forced the American government out of Lebanon in a spectacular coup and the Providence Liberation Army of Palestine would never again want for money or supplies, because once again they had proven that they had enough power to influence the policies of entire governments.

The telephone rang. "It is done," said the voice on the other end. "I have received a transmission from Atlanta. Abu has completed his assignment. Thirty-two dead, another twenty wounded."

"This is very good, Raad, my loyal friend," Tahril answered, sitting down behind a desk in the corner of the room. "What of Galla? Has she begun?"

There was a second of silence. "She was to make contact an hour ago but I have heard nothing."

Tahril frowned. "Have you telephoned the apartment?"

"Yes. The receiver is lifted but she does not respond when I speak. I was afraid to say too much in case —"

Tahril leaned forward. "What *did* you say?"

"I said only — hello Galla, is this you?"

Ahmed Tahril brought his fleshy fist down on the desk top. "She has betrayed us," he roared, his voice rising an octave. "No one is to be there. She was to associate with no one. And now someone else is picking up her telephone?" His full cheeks quivered with rage. "Kill her."

"But we cannot be sure. Something may have happened."

"Exactly. She may have been discovered. Galla Attawa was trained in the camps, Raad. She can provide them with Intelligence they do not have. This is why she must die. But do not feel badly, my friend, Galla was prepared for death."

* * * * *

It was to be a celebration, congratulations for a successful operation, arranged long distance by

Ahmed Tahril. Two Palestinian women had come into the house to prepare the food, and a brooding teenage boy with bare legs and battered tennis shoes served the meal to the group at the dining room table.

Madison hated herself for having an appetite, hated her stomach for growling in the wake of the embassy bombing. But she did her best to justify her hunger. She had eaten nothing but a few grapes and she must maintain her strength, she told herself furiously.

Max seemed to deal with it the same way he always dealt with anything unpleasant: he simply refused to think about it until he could take the time to reason it out. Madison admired that in him, admired his patience.

Yael was happy because she truly believed in her revolution, believed that their bombs were detonated for a good and noble cause. Madison pitied her for that, pitied the fact that it had taken the deaths of so many to bring a smile to Yael's face. One day Yael Chazan would have to pay for her hatred.

And Michael: Michael was just Michael, who always seemed to be happy, and Madison envied and hated that in him all at once.

The sulky teenage boy first filled the wine glasses then delivered three steaming dishes to the center of the table. Max leaned forward and peered into one of the dishes suspiciously, and then in his completely loveable and unpretentious way asked, "What in the world is it?"

"Lamb cooked with dill seed and mushrooms," Yael answered. "And this, my friends, is our main course, a Middle Eastern specialty called *Imam*

Bayildi. It means The Priest Fainted. It is said that many years ago a great holy man was so overcome by the delicious aroma that he fainted at his table when it was first served to him."

Max, enchanted by Yael's story, looked at his food with renewed interest. But Michael Peelor merely shrugged and mumbled that it was really just stuffed eggplant. To this Max objected loudly. "You've done it now, Michael, taken every bit of the romance right out of the meal for me."

Everyone laughed, except Madison who simply smiled and pretended to be amused. In her mind, she was still sitting in the gold Honda, staring blankly as the young driver prepared himself for death and slammed his lethal load into the front of the embassy. She was still fighting back images of horrified faces as melting street lights dripped on hot pavement

"Madison," Yael said, abruptly. "I owe you an apology. What I saw in your eyes today could not have been insincere. I am sorry I have not trusted you."

Madison nodded. "Apology accepted."

Max had lost his smile and was staring at his fork for lack of a better place to rest his eyes. Michael's clear grey eyes darted back and forth between Yael and Madison as the women looked at each other. Then, as if they had rehearsed their lines for awkward situations, Michael and Max exchanged glances, and said in unison, "Let's eat."

After dinner Yael wandered off into the living room to watch the television news which was

162

entirely dedicated to the embassy bombing. She leaned back in the sofa cushions and stared at the screen, reveling in the magnificence of Providence's bloody victory

Disgusted, Madison borrowed a cigarette from Michael Peelor, and moved outside onto the deck where she stood watching the lights twinkling along the coast. Here, she thought, with the warm night air against her face and the smell of salty water, with the lights glistening along the beach, she might have been anywhere, in any house, on any coastline. It could have been Lisbon or Cartagena or Marseille . . . it could have been Buxton, North Carolina, and Terry could be standing behind her, arms threaded under her arms, head resting against Madison's shoulder blades. She sighed and closed her eyes. Then a burst of light in the distance interrupted her darkness, then the sound of gunfire. She opened her eyes to the reality and chaos that was Beirut, Lebanon.

Max stepped out onto the deck and closed the glass doors behind him. His pipe clenched between his teeth, he leaned forward and rested his big hands on the railing. "You okay?" he asked, staring straight ahead.

Madison, embarrassed by the tear that had found its way to her cheek, was grateful that he had chosen not to look at her. "You know, I was going to quit smoking today," she announced, casually using her sleeve to wipe away the tear, "but I suppose I've just been doing it too long."

Max still did not look at her. "I'm leavin', Madi. I'm leavin' as soon as I can figure a way out. Can't do this."

"What about Mossad?" she whispered. "What about the money? What about the operation?"

"The money has already been deposited. And screw the bloody operation." Still leaning on the railing, he turned to her. "I told myself I was doin' it for the money. Then I told myself I was doin' it cause it was the right thing. Well, you know what that got me? It got me buildin' a bloody detonator that helped kill sixty somethin' people. I swear I didn't know it. It was just a simple little operation, they told me. I didn't know the whole fuckin' truck was loaded with TNT. Eight hundred pounds of the stuff. And if I would have known, I'm not sure I'd have had the gonads to say no. I can live with this. I'm good at that, you know. I'll find a way to excuse myself, I'll justify it, all right. But I can't keep doin' it."

Madison wrapped an arm around his back and leaned against his big chest. "Am I invited to the wedding?"

Max gave the top of her head a gentle kiss. "Go with me, Madi. Walk away from this mess once and for all."

"I can't, Max. I just can't."

"Come on, we've both seen a hundred operations like this, and not one of them ever made a difference in the long run. This war will outlive the both of us. Can't you see there's no solution, no end comin'? You give your whole life to the Company and you know what you'll have when they're done with you? You'll have yourself, Madi, nothin' more. This is not your war."

"Max, this isn't about the Palestinian uprising or Israeli security. It's about losing our freedom because we're afraid to step on a plane or sit our children in an airport lobby. This war is about terrorism, and terrorism is wrong, Max, no matter which side plans it, no matter which side administers it."

Max looked down at her. "Even when the U.S. does it, Madi? Is it still wrong in your eyes then?"

Madison's green eyes locked on him for a moment. "This is not open for debate, Max," she said quietly, then turned and left him standing alone on the deck.

Max shook his head and complained to himself, "Blasted inflexible, flag wavin' woman. That's what she is all right."

CHAPTER TWELVE

Dent Webb, the first man of color to become Director of the Federal Bureau of Investigation and the first FBI Director to end what traditionally had been an uncooperative relationship between the FBI and the CIA, unbuttoned his jacket and loosened his tie as he sat down across from Mitchell Colby in Colby's spacious Langley office.

"I'm up to my ass in alligators, Mitchell," said Webb, his deepset brown eyes resting on the CIA Director. "Attawa finally talked. She informed my men she was sent here to blow up an American jetliner flying within our borders."

"What flight?"

Leaning back and crossing his long legs, Dent Webb took a breath and blew it out slowly. "It didn't matter. The point was to attack from within. Listen to this." He extracted a sheet of paper from his inside coat pocket. "We will expose the weaknesses of this government to its people."

Mitchell Colby popped an antacid tablet into his mouth and tucked it in his cheek. "What else did she say?"

"Nothing. Not a damn thing. The only reason she talked at all was simply to terrorize us in the only way she knows how without the help of guns or bombs. We don't know how many others have penetrated our borders, or who her controller is here in the States. Her telephone records led us to a public telephone in Manhattan. We traced the plastic explosive to a Czech manufacturer, but she won't say how she purchased it in New York or if she carried it over with her . . . We covered up the school yard shooting, but if this kind of thing happens again I'm not sure we can keep a lid on it."

Colby was scribbling something on a note pad. "Where is she now?"

"A safe house outside Albany."

Mitchell Colby pushed out his thick lips. "Let's get her to our medical facility in Fairfax. We'll get some answers out of her there."

Dent Webb could not disguise his surprise. "You mean chemicals?" Webb stood and began pacing the length of the office, hands on his hips, head down.

Colby sat there calmly, silently, watching Dent Webb's long strides take him around the office like an expectant father in a hospital waiting room. "Let's be frank here, shall we," Colby said at length. "You're going to lose your job unless you can control the situation."

Webb stopped and spun around. "Whose side are you on here?"

"It's not a question of taking sides. I'm trying to save your ass. It's your agency's job to protect the country from this type of infiltration, and frankly your agency wasn't able to perform in this case. Now I know that isn't your fault. I happen to believe you're the best damn Director the FBI has ever seen. But you're right, you know, if we have another strike in this country you won't be able to cover it up and people will be looking to you for answers. We need whatever information she has, and Galla Attawa forfeited her rights when she came into this country with the express purpose of taking innocent lives. In my opinion we have the responsibility to get some answers from her by any means possible."

Colby smiled and leaned forward, elbows propped on his desk. "You're in the big leagues now. You'll have to learn how to cover your ass while you get the job done. You can't pee-pee with the pups if you want to run with the big dogs."

Dent Webb sat down. "And the big dogs in Washington cover their backsides by violating basic human rights."

"We do what we have to do to protect this great country. And you, my friend, aren't going to be able to participate in that process if you're the *former* Director of the FBI."

* * * * *

Madison McGuire sat in the driver's seat of the gold Honda waiting for Max to return from his rendezvous with his Israeli controller. It was their first taste of freedom, their first time away from Michael Peelor or Yael Chazan, and Madison wasn't sure what kind of reception she would receive if she returned without Max. And it seemed very likely that Max would not return. At this very moment he was making arrangements for safe passage out of Lebanon.

Parked in a damaged section of downtown Beirut, she looked up at the tall concrete apartment building next to her. The damage was so extensive that nearly half of the balconies appeared ready to fall, the massive steel cables that supported them exposed, the balconies leaning dangerously towards the street.

Two women stood on the corner, waiting to cross. One, carrying a child in her arms, wore a tattered black dress made for a woman twice her size. Her legs were bare and bruised, her feet laboring to support heavy men's sandals. The woman beside her was short and pear-shaped, and wore the same type of dress and carried a bag of groceries. So casual was the manner in which they carried out their daily routines, they could have been any pair of women in any part of the world taking a midday stroll. The almost constant sound of gunfire that rang out in some part of the city every day was no more than background noise, the concrete and rubble in the streets no more than a minor obstacle to be stepped over as they moved towards their destination. After all, they were the experts at living with war, the veterans who had lived it and breathed it every day of their lives in a part of the world where no one was truly a civilian.

Madison wondered vaguely what type of person she might have become had she been born Israeli or Palestinian or Lebanese, Muslim or Jew. And then she cursed herself and all her prejudices as she watched the women cross the street, as she attempted to measure the differences between her world and theirs. Like them, she had become accustomed to war, desensitized by the horrors of it. But they, she mused, were the noble ones. The ones who had innocently been thrown into the fighting and learned to smile and build lives and raise families in spite of it.

Max appeared, lumbering up the war-torn block towards the car, his face heated and sweaty from the hot Mediterranean sun. He slapped the hood of the car loudly as he neared the driver's window, apparently for no other reason than to get a laugh out of startling Madison.

"It's all set, old girl. You handle your end and we'll both be sittin' pretty. When they find out I was a Mossad plant they'll be in a hurry to get out, and it seems logical they'd head for the camps. I get to go home and you get a look at the camps . . . I'm gonna miss you, love. You shoot straight now, Madi, and keep yourself safe. I'll be expectin' to hear from you soon."

Madison stepped out of the car and wrapped her arms around his big neck. "Soon," she answered, giving him a kiss and then climbing back in the car. She had never been one for long goodbyes.

Max pulled a Beretta M9, 9mm semi-automatic pistol from his belt and handed it to her through the car window. "You might be needin' this." He stroked his bushy mustache and looked at Madison as if trying to remember what it was he wanted to say. He asked casually after several seconds of concentrated hesitation, "Want me to call Terry? Give her a message?"

Madison smiled gratefully. "Tell her I'm safe. Oh, and Max, I love you."

He patted her hand and stepped back as she drove away.

* * * * *

Special Agent Kevin Pierce hung up the telephone in the Albany, New York, safe house. "That's it. We're supposed to take her to the airstrip right away. Director's orders. They want her in Fairfax for questioning. Hope they do better than we did," he added to his partner, heading towards the room where Galla Attawa was being held.

"I'll pull the car around," answered agent Ellen Case, a serious young woman who had passed her final exams at Quantico only eighteen months before and had got herself assigned to the counter-intelligence section of the Federal Bureau of Investigation only six months ago.

Galla Attawa sat sullenly on the bed in a plainly furnished room that was in sharp contrast to the cheerfully decorated safe house where she had been kept. "All right, it's time to go. You're not going to make this hard on me, are you, Galla? I'm going to have to cuff you."

"Where are you taking me?" Attawa demanded.

"The Director would like to meet you," Pierce answered while he snapped the handcuffs on her wrists. "Let's go."

They were almost at the front door when she spun around and looked at Pierce. "They'll never let you take me. We have people here. We have our spies too. They'll know where I am."

"Is that right?" Agent Pierce responded with a grin. "Well you can tell it all to the head office. I'm sure they'll be fascinated."

Holding Attawa firmly, one hand grasping her forearm, he cracked the door and looked outside. It was a dark, rainy day, a slow, continuous drizzle falling on the run-down residential street.

When she saw the front door open, Agent Case reached back and pushed open the back door of the dark blue Buick. Kevin Pierce surveyed the street once more before shoving Attawa out the door in front of him.

The first thought that crossed his mind was that she had lost her balance somehow, tripped on a pebble or a shoelace. Then as he knelt beside her, he saw the blood mingling with the rain on the sidewalk, and the small hole in her shirt. He hit the ground at once and started moving towards the car on his stomach. Agent Ellen Case, seeing what had happened but hearing nothing at all, flattened herself in the front seat and began working her way towards the passenger door. By now their weapons were drawn, by now both agents had seen the man behind the tree across the street with the silenced rifle and scope pointed toward them.

Case rolled out of the car and quickly positioned

herself behind it. Pierce raised and fired once then ducked back down. "There's only one. I'm going to try and get behind him," he told her. "Cover me."

Ellen Case raised herself up slightly, aimed towards the tree and opened fire as Kevin Pierce darted off to the left. The tactic was not lost on the sniper. Pierce made it perhaps twenty feet before taking the first bullet. A second and then a third followed. Agent Case watched Pierce fall, watched his body jerk with each bullet, watched the rain begin to soak through his clothing as he lay still in the grass. She leaned against the car, her breathing heavy, irregular. She had been trained extensively, but this was her first live combat situation, and it was these few seconds of indecision that kept her from later providing her agency with the plate number of the vehicle that raced by and picked up the sniper. By the time she attempted to raise up again, the man was already in the vehicle firing in her direction, preventing her from returning the fire or getting a good look at their faces. Those few seconds of indecision and the deaths of Special Agent Kevin Pierce and Galla Attawa later cost Ellen Case her position in the Counter-Intelligence section; she was assigned indefinitely to the Albuquerque, New Mexico, office.

* * * * *

A wrong turn, an unfamiliar street. Madison slowed and looked around, remembering her first day in Beirut. Peelor had told her the East-West seaside road ran from Beirut to Damascus and past the wealthy area where Ahmed Tahril kept a home. She turned right, onto a side street, believing it would take her towards the only landmark she could identify in the strange city, the water.

The street began to narrow, the white concrete buildings showing more damage. Just ahead the street was blocked by concrete blocks and lumber. A glimpse of a man walking around a corner, an automatic weapon slung over his shoulder, made it frightfully clear to Madison that she had entered the heavily guarded southern slums of Beirut, the part of the city that had been bombed during the 1982 Israeli invasion, a section now occupied by some of the more radical Shi'ite Muslim groups. Quickly she pulled onto another side street and, seeing what faced her, slammed on the brakes and threw the car into reverse.

Two young men with ammunition belts stretched across their upper bodies and Israeli-made Uzi's in their hands were running towards her, shouting in a language she did not understand. By the time she rammed the car into first gear, one of the two was standing in front of the car, the submachine gun pointed at the windshield.

"Shit," she muttered, looking down at the Levis and expensive running shoes she wore; both would identify her as a Westerner.

The second man came from behind the car and approached the driver's side. He was shouting something at her, his black eyes wild. Madison felt the Beretta M9 under her leg, felt some security in its presence, though her heart was racing.

He was more insistent now, yelling louder in very poor English, opening the driver's door. "Papers. Where are your papers?"

Madison held up her left hand in surrender and slowly reached for the identification she had been given and handed him the fake passport that identified her as Diane Delaney from Ireland. He carried it to the man standing in front of the car, Uzi still pointed at the windshield. They studied the passport, occasionally looking up at Madison, while she covertly removed the 9mm from under her leg and placed it next to the seat, her right hand gripping it.

With the submachine gun still pointed at the window, the two men seemed to be engaged in a discussion, and Madison knew it was her future they were deciding. So many thoughts rushed through her mind. How many hostages had been seized in exactly the same manner? How many people now lived in captivity simply because they had taken a wrong turn in a Middle Eastern country? And could she take them both with the automatic pistol before they had time to return the fire? Her palm began to sweat and her throat became dry as she tightened her grip on the Beretta and slowly brought it to her lap in preparation.

Then the Uzi was lowered and the English-speaking Shi'ite yelled to her, "You know IRA?"

Madison put the pistol back beside the seat, but did not release it, and with a nod she repeated, "IRA," and smiled.

The two men laughed, and the one who had been pointing the Uzi at her windshield elbowed the other, whispered something and began walking back down the alley. Madison breathed a sigh of relief.

The remaining man returned to the car. He was

young, twenty perhaps, wore khaki pants and a dirty white shirt. He had slung his weapon back over his shoulder, apparently deciding that an Irish woman was not his enemy, particularly not a woman who smiled at the mention of the Irish Republican Army.

He crouched beside the car, the driver's door still open, and spoke to her with a smile. "You want me, pretty?"

"I don't understand," Madison lied, for she did understand all too well what his question implied.

Still smiling, he touched her face and slowly ran a finger down her neck towards her breasts. Madison brought her left arm up sharply and blocked him. His smile faded. He grabbed her arm and jerked her from the car with one hand, the other hand popping the snap on her jeans and tugging at the zipper.

She had held onto the pistol on her way out of the car, and as he twisted her left wrist brutally and ripped open the zipper, one filthy hand working its way into her pants, she pressed the 9mm into his stomach and squeezed the trigger.

His black eyes froze on hers before he dropped to the ground.

Madison stood over him, tears of rage running down her cheeks. "This is for all the women," she whispered, then fired again. And in her fury, if she could have killed him twice, if she could have inflicted more pain on him, she would have kept firing.

The other man had heard the loud report of the Beretta and was running towards her now, firing the Uzi, bullets screaming, tearing up the pavement in front of her. She waited calmly for him to come into range, her anger mounting. Another twenty yards

. . . then ten . . . She fired and watched without emotion as the bullet ripped open his neck.

Two hundred yards down the street she saw more of them running towards her. Quickly, she grabbed the Uzi lying beside the dead man and sprayed the street, forcing the group to scatter, buying enough time to climb into the car. Slamming it into gear, she lowered the electric window on the passenger side and opened up with the Uzi once again before spinning the wheels and heading north out of Beirut's southern slums.

* * * * *

Greg Allen Abbott walked into the Director's seventh floor office carrying a stack of satellite photographs under his arm like a schoolboy carried his books. "Good morning, sir."

"I understand you've really been putting in the hours downstairs. Hope my people are cooperating. They're not accustomed to working with people from other agencies, you know."

"They're putting up with me," Abbott offered with a bright smile. "I've been going over the photos of the Bekaa Valley camps and I think I've noticed some increased activity at camp number four-fifty-six. The infrared pictures from a week ago show heat coming from only two of the twelve huts. Last night's pictures show heat in five."

"Well, it's good to be aware of these things. Even if camp four-fifty-six isn't the Providence camps, some other group may be gearing up for an operation. Let's have a look."

As Abbott handed the photographs over the desk

to the Director, and the Director began pushing aside the many folders and papers on his desk, Abbott caught a glimpse of a file folder marked *Bluebird—Eyes Only*. Momentarily paralyzed, he simply stared at the folder, unable to move.

Mitchell Colby looked at Abbott and then followed his stare to the folder. "What is it, son?"

Abbott shook his head. "I'm not sure. It's just that that name is so familiar. I've seen it somewhere, typed just like that."

Colby frowned. "Remember where you saw it?"

"No, sir. I'm sorry."

After Greg Abbott had left the Director's office, Mitchell Colby summoned his Deputy Directors to his office and issued them instructions to begin surveillance on anyone who had had contact with Greg Abbott since the planning of Operation White Flag began.

Greg Abbott moved like a sleepwalker back to the fourth floor cubicle the CIA had loaned him. Where had he seen the word Bluebird, he asked himself. What was significant about the word? He found a dictionary and looked it up. A songbird, it said, mostly blue in color. He sat down and scribbled the word several times on a note pad, but it was no help.

* * * * *

In Christian East Beirut, Michael Peelor and Yael Chazan sat in the converted garage, Yael at the computer and Michael speaking into a scrambled telephone line. "No. They went into town an hour or so ago."

"For what reason?" Ahmed Tahril inquired.

"Just a few personal items. They're old friends, you know. I think they wanted some time to themselves. Besides, there's nothing going on here, and no one knows their faces. I figured it was safe enough."

"I see," Tahril answered pensively. "How did she respond to yesterday's operation?"

Michael Peelor smiled, remembering the look in Madison's cool green eyes after the embassy bombing. "Like a pro. The woman is really something, Ahmed. Even Yael is satisfied, and Yael doesn't trust anyone, myself included." He glanced at Yael and smiled.

"I need you to leave for the training center in two days. We have new recruits coming in next week. Drive the car as far as Zahlah and I'll have someone pick you up."

"Whatever you say, boss. What about Yael and Madison?"

"I'm making arrangements for them to go to Tel Aviv for an operation, if Madison has decided to work with us. I think we proved our ability to her yesterday. I want all of you to stay in the house until it's time to leave. If you need anything I'll have it brought to you. You did a brilliant job, Michael. I'll be in touch. You know how to reach me in case of an emergency."

"Yes, sir." Peelor turned to Yael. "Our fearless leader sends his praises." He paused. "I think I hear the car." They both walked to the front door and opened it just as Madison was about to turn the doorknob. Yael gasped at the sight of the zipper hanging out of Madison's jeans, the swollen left wrist, the wild, violent stare. They were both so concerned by Madison's appearance and the story she told them about the Shi'ite group and the attempted rape, that it wasn't until Yael had iced Madison's wrist and sat her on the couch that it occurred to Peelor that Max was not with her.

"He said he'd be back later," Madison told them. "He wanted to visit an old friend. If the bloody fool had been with me I never would have gotten lost." She grimaced as Yael adjusted the ice pack on the sore wrist.

Peelor and Yael exchanged glances. "Where exactly did you leave him?" Peelor asked.

"Did you see this friend of his? Would you recognize him if you saw him again? What did he look like?" Yael grilled her.

"Yes, I saw him. What' the problem?"

Michael Peelor rubbed his scruffy chin. "Max told us he had never been here. He said he didn't know anyone in Beirut."

Madison took a cigarette from his pack. "What exactly are you saying, Michael?"

"I'm saying that we may have a big problem."

"And you, Madison," Yael piped in, releasing the ice pack, "may have an even bigger problem. You are the one that did not return with our explosives man."

"Are you suggesting that I'm a spy, Yael?" Madison snapped. "You think I took Max and turned him over to the authorities? That is utterly ridiculous," Madison said, dismissing her with a wave of her hand.

"All right, let's not panic," Peelor broke in, looking at Yael. "If Madison was a plant then why

180

would she risk coming back without Max? It would be a hell of a lot smarter for her to get out and send the authorities here for us. We wouldn't expect it. An American team could have just as easily been standing at that door . . . It's Rudger I'm worried about."

"Come now, Michael. Surely you don't believe Max is working undercover," Madison said. "Maybe he just wanted some time to himself, for chrissake. I think you're jumping to conclusions here."

Michael Peelor walked to the office. Madison and Yael followed. He plugged the scrambling device into the telephone and made a call. It took Madison only a few seconds to realize that he was speaking with Ahmed Tahril, telling him the story and giving him the address where Madison had left the Irishman.

Fifteen minutes later the telephone rang and the fax machine began to hum. Tahril was on the line again, and Peelor, cradling the phone on his shoulder, ripped a sheet from the fax machine and handed it to Madison. "Is this the man you saw Max talking to?"

Madison studied it. "Yes."

Peelor sat down and spoke into the telephone quietly, then muttered, "Damn it."

Madison jerked the phone from his hand. "Mr. Tahril, it's Madison. What's going on?"

"You have just delivered our new explosives man to an Israeli agent, Madison. What is your explanation, please?"

"I don't believe it," Madison murmured.

"Believe it," Tahril's smooth voice answered. "The photograph corresponds with Libyan Intelligence files. Max Rudger is working for the Mossad. His

181

controller, Shulmel Berglass, is a man that has caused us great difficulty in the past."

Madison was silent for a few seconds. "I want Max. And I want him before he has time to do any real damage. How much time do you think we have before Mossad shows up?"

Tahril smiled. "I knew you wouldn't disappoint us, Madison. I had a feeling about you."

"How much time?" Madison demanded.

"Twenty-four hours, perhaps. I'm going to have to cancel our immediate operational plans and make arrangements to get you all out of Beirut."

"Not until you let me have Max. I've had enough betrayal to last a lifetime. He set us up, he's going to have to pay."

"I understand. You'll have your chance, my new friend. It must be done and I certainly have no objection to you doing it. Now, please, let me speak to Michael."

Madison handed the telephone to Michael Peelor and walked out of the office. She stood at the kitchen cabinet and smiled as she poured herself a congratulatory shot of the scotch she had found in the kitchen the day before. This performance could earn her an Oscar, she mused with satisfaction.

CHAPTER THIRTEEN

Shulmel Berglass peered out the sixth floor window of the downtown Beirut apartment building, then turned to Max Rudger who sat patiently in the main room of the shabby apartment on an old worn chair, smoking his pipe. "A gold Honda?" Berglass inquired.

"That's right. They here?"

"Three of them, sitting across the street from the main entrance. I hope your friend's aim is as good as you say."

Max stood, and smiled with more ease than he

felt. "Can't speak for the others, but Madison could trim my mustache from that distance. Hope whoever has been assigned to you is as accurate."

The Israeli agent looked at Max with obvious uncertainty. Max patted him on the back. "Take it easy, old man. It's a good plan. We get ourselves out of this mess and Madison does the work for us." He walked to the window and peeked out. "Think we should let them wait a while?"

"Yes," Berglass answered nervously. "If we walk out too soon it may seem strange."

"All right then, enough time for another beer is what I say."

Berglass, watching Max casually take a beer from the tiny icebox, shook his head. He had still not decided whether Max Rudger was the bravest man he had ever known or merely the most insane.

Outside, Madison sat in the passenger seat of the gold Honda holding Max's Beretta in her lap. Peelor and Yael had both inquired as to how she had managed to obtain the weapon, and Madison had told them truthfully, "Max gave it to me." Minutes later she had found them checking it to be sure it carried live ammunition.

Now, sitting in the car in the center of Beirut with the tall buildings choking off the breeze and the afternoon sun beating down into the car, the strangeness of it all seemed to overwhelm her, and with rare openness she told them quietly, "You know, I've done some very questionable things in my lifetime. I've photographed innocent people in the name of national security. I've listened in on private conversations and submitted my reports in invisible ink. I've played secret games and been trained to

184

speak a dozen languages so I could infiltrate foreign countries and turn unfortunate citizens into paid informants. But I've never ever waited on a downtown street to shoot my best friend."

Yael touched her shoulder gently. "You wouldn't be human if you didn't question yourself at times. But you must remember that your best friend has betrayed you, and betrayal has a price."

Madison sensed Yael's obsession once again, and was once again frightened by it. I am her friend, Madison thought, now that I will kill for her cause.

A figure was emerging from the tall concrete apartment building. He was short and stocky, with black hair and mustache.

"That's Berglass," Michael Peelor whispered from the back seat, and then Madison saw Max coming out behind his controller.

"Can you take him, Madison? I'll get the Israeli," Peelor announced, and Madison heard the clip on his semi-automatic snap into place.

Holding the Beretta in both hands, Madison nodded, and Peelor waited until both men were in clear view to give the command. "Now."

The sound was deafening inside the car as Madison fired twice at Max's chest, trying to ignore the pain that shot through her swollen wrist from the Beretta's heavy recoil.

Max Rudger's feet came out from under him and he flipped over backwards. The Israeli agent was already on the ground, hit several times by Peelor's fire.

"Get it, Yael," Peelor ordered, and Yael hit the gas, wheels screeching, as they made their escape.

Moments later Max Rudger picked himself up off

the ground and opened his shirt, looking at the marks in the bulletproof vest. He frowned and rubbed his chest. "Felt like she used a bleedin' cannon," he mumbled, and walked towards his Israeli controller. "Berglass, get up, old man."

Shulmel Berglass groaned, "I'm hit."

"Where?" Then Max saw the blood running from his upper arm. "Let's take a look-see." He ripped open the shirt and smiled. "You're going to live, my friend. Nothing we can't fix up."

After helping Berglass to his feet, Max brushed himself off and looked down the street. "Goodbye, Madi, my love. Be safe."

*　*　*　*　*

The group returned to the house only long enough to retrieve their clothes and a few personal items. Michael Peelor brought along an ounce of Lebanese hashish, Madison grabbed her toothbrush and a book from Tahril's bookshelf entitled *The West Bank Story*, and Yael took fruit from the refrigerator and stuffed it into a paper bag.

On the way out of Beirut, Michael insisted that they stop and have a Lebanese doctor examine Madison's wrist. She felt a bit like a child when she stepped out of the examination room, her wrist wrapped and supported by a sling, to find Yael and Michael waiting there like concerned parents.

"It's a severe sprain. Very painful at times, but it will heal quickly," the doctor told them. His nurse came out and whispered into his ear. He frowned and looked at the strange group as if he were searching for his next words. "My assistant informs

186

me that a jeep filled with Israeli soldiers has just pulled up outside."

"Holy shit," Peelor declared, yanking a curtain to look.

"You are in trouble?"

"Yes, doctor," Madison answered, sensing his willingness to help. "Do you have a vehicle? We have money."

"If your trouble is with the Israelis you do not need money here. My car is in the rear of the building. A brown BMW. Hurry, please," he pleaded, directing them through his small offices and out the rear exit. "Go to the right, then left. You will be heading east."

Peelor paused before climbing into the driver's seat. "What will you say?"

The doctor smiled. "I will say you are all thieves, that you took my old white Mercedes."

With only the clothes on their backs, the money in their pockets, one ounce of hashish, and the gun Michael Peelor had stuck in the back of his pants, the group left Beirut and headed east towards the safety of Lebanon's Syrian-controlled Bekaa Valley.

* * * * *

With a painting of Lenin staring down at him and a diplomatic passport in his back pocket, Nikolai Mikhailovich Orstroklova sat at his Soviet Embassy desk in Washington, D.C., and read the decoded message from KGB headquarters, Moscow. He felt the noose of his superiors tightening around his neck as he read their panicked demands for more Intelligence. He imagined himself being shipped back to Moscow because he could not satisfy the demands for faster, deeper Intelligence on American activities, imagined walking the city's grimy streets, passing the dull, unsmiling Muscovites who hadn't yet had an opportunity to experience the "new openness" that the rest of the world seemed so hopeful about.

Nikolai crumpled the message and tossed it into the red trash can which was reserved for secret documents, its contents emptied, shredded and incinerated every two hours. He sighed as he tapped his fingers nervously on the desk top. What in the hell had happened? Why was he taking the heat for Yuri Vissarionovich Kaski's disappearance some four thousand miles away in Frankfurt, Germany? Which of his superiors, in all their wisdom, had decided that Yuri Kaski had defected to the American side? Which of them had come to the startling conclusion that since Nikolai's agent, Bluebird, had been the last one to pass information that directly affected Kaski, somehow Bluebird was involved in the alleged defection? They believed that the message relayed by Katherine Maloane concerning a retired agent named Scorpion must have been a code telling Kaski he could come over, defect.

Chaos had erupted within the Kremlin. As the senior European Intelligence officer, and a KGB Colonel, Yuri Kaski could provide American Intelligence with enough information on KGB operations, methods and Soviet technology to throw Soviet-American relations back into the Cold War. Nikolai grunted at the thought. Had the Cold War ever truly ended? If so, he mused, someone had certainly neglected to inform the Intelligence agencies of the Soviet Union and the United States of America.

The message that now lay in the bottom of the red trash can had been very clear. KGB headquarters wanted to know about Yuri Kaski. Nikolai was instructed to dig deeper, use every source, every informant until the truth could be known. They had to know what the Americans knew, had to be prepared to tear down networks and break off contact with informants who could be exposed as spies.

Perhaps Bluebird *did* have the answers, he reflected. Bluebird who had always been a bit too eager and too easily bought. Bluebird who would betray her country and sleep with him for an envelope filled with cash. Bluebird who converted her profits to white powder and sucked them up her nose. Bluebird who was suddenly unable to provide him with accurate Intelligence.

Nikolai Mikhailovich Orstroklova leaned back in his chair and mumbled, "You are a whore, my Bluebird, of this I am sure. But are you also a double agent? We shall soon find out."

CHAPTER FOURTEEN

The fertile, intensively cultivated land that ran between Beirut on the coast and the Anti-Lebanon Mountains on the Syrian border was sprinkled with small limestone farmhouses with red tiled roofs, and clusters of women, men and children working the fields. Rich farmland and plush green fields rushed by as Madison McGuire, Michael Peelor and Yael Chazan drove east towards the Lebanon Mountains, over the rolling countryside and through tiny villages where men still gathered in the main square for entertainment and gossip, and women huddled together and spoke in quiet, reverent tones.

They had made only one stop since the journey began. A Toyota jeep had been waiting for them in a small town called Alayh, where they bought food, changed vehicles and parked on the edge of town to eat.

Madison watched a group of young boys playing. They held their sticks like guns and played the game they had seen their fathers and older brothers playing for years. She watched a small boy sneak up behind a group of his friends, leave a paper bag on the ground next to them, and then run for cover. Seconds later he raised his head and shouted something to the group.

"What is he saying?" Madison asked.

Michael Peelor wiped his mouth with his sleeve and smiled. "He's telling them they're all dead, there was a grenade in the bag. He'll make a good soldier one day."

"Ten or fifteen years ago," Yael added nostalgically, "before the Civil War here, those children might have been playing soccer or hide-and-go-seek. Now they play at war. It is what they see and hear. Words of war, weapons of war. It is what they know."

"Kids all over the world play war, Yael," Michael answered. "I played war when I was a kid."

"Yes, I suppose all *boys* play war games. But were you as proficient at it as they are? Just look at them."

Michael shook his head and smiled. "Oh, I get it. You're trying to say it's always the men and boys who play war games. Is that it? I've seen you toss your share of grenades too. Don't forget that."

Yael turned to face him. "Women have to fight. We have no choice. We live in a world of men who start wars."

Madison smiled and Michael looked at her. "You want in on any of this male-bashing? I want you both to get it all out of your systems before we get on the road again. I don't think I can stand another four hours of this."

Madison stretched out in the back of the jeep. "Four hours wouldn't be long enough, my friend," she answered, with a wink in Yael's direction.

* * * * *

"My God, it's beautiful," Madison said, sitting up from her nap and seeing the rolling land before her and the snow-capped mountains in the distance.

"Welcome to the land of the *Al Biqa*. Better known as the Bekaa Valley," Michael answered cheerfully. "Farmers still thresh their grain with an ox and a handmade shaft here. And just a little south are the most sophisticated training camps for freedom fighters in the world. It's a trip."

Yael's eyes were fixed on Michael. She was smiling a strange, distant smile. "Jesus, Yael, what the hell is it?" Peelor asked uncomfortably.

"Freedom fighters," she muttered. "I like that."

Michael Peelor rolled his eyes and smiled at Madison, but Yael didn't see. She was looking off into the distance. "Look, there are the camps," she announced excitedly. "See them, Madison? We are safe here."

Madison looked out the window at the rows of ugly aluminum huts cluttering a beautiful, lush green meadow. *You are safe until I betray you. That is what I do, Yael. I befriend and then I betray.*

* * * * *

Greg Allen Abbott sat straight up from a sound sleep, his eyes wide, his skin glistening with perspiration. An hour later he was knocking on the front door of the Director of Central Intelligence.

It was barely dawn. The two men walked through the shimmering dew-coated grass towards a small pond several hundred yards from the main house, side by side like father and son, Colby a full head taller, and Abbott half his width.

The Director, rumpled and puffy from being shaken out of bed after a late-night dinner party, had stopped once along the way to take a breath, stretch his arms and attempt to touch his toes. He mentioned to Abbott that he sometimes visited this place in the evenings when the lights from D.C. danced in the distance and tinted the sky yellow and orange.

"It's a great city, Washington," he told Abbott, and it crossed Abbott's mind that the world must seem cleaner and newer when one has the advantage of seeing it at a distance.

"I'm sorry to disturb you so early. Please apologize to Mrs. Colby."

The Director waved a hand and grunted. "That woman walks the floors half the night anyway. She's like a damn ghost." He sat down on a wooden bench and leaned forward, tossing a pebble into the pond. "I assume this is about White Flag."

Abbott sat down next to him. "Actually, no. It's about Bluebird . . . I have to know about Bluebird."

Colby leaned back slowly and gave Abbott a sideways glance. "You're not cleared for Bluebird. Just tell me what's on your mind."

Abbott's words were slow, measured. "I may have information about Bluebird. But I have to know what Bluebird *is* before I know what to make of it. The problem is it concerns someone . . . ah . . . someone at State. Naturally I don't want to name names until I fully understand what the implications may be."

Colby leaned over again and picked up another rock. "So you remembered where you saw the name," he said, throwing the rock into the water.

"Yes," Abbott answered quietly. "I need to know what to do with the information. If there's a problem in the State Department, I owe it to the Secretary to make him aware of the problem before it goes any further."

"You're loyal. That's good." Colby smiled kindly. "I'll give you my personal guarantee that the Secretary will be advised before any action is taken."

Abbott shook his head. "I appreciate that, sir, but I have to know what it means for myself."

"So, you're involved with this person. A friend or lover?"

"Friend," Abbott responded.

Colby was silent for several moments, but it was not an uncomfortable silence, for Mitchell Colby had a thoughtfulness about him that made one feel secure during his lapses into quiet.

"Bluebird is a Soviet code name. If you've seen the word written in someone's office, on someone's desk calendar, in someone's briefcase, chances are you've uncovered the person we've been looking for for almost a year now. Bluebird is a spy, a traitor who's been selling classified information to the Soviets, and probably the one who's responsible for tipping the Soviet agent to McGuire's arrival in Frankfurt. Our asset in Moscow uncovered the code name months ago. If this thing pans out, son, you're going to be a big star in Washington."

Colby put his arm around Abbott and patted him on the shoulder. They sat quietly on the bench for several minutes, as if all the talk of treason had somehow created a fellowship between them.

"What will happen when I turn over the name?" Abbott asked at length.

"Well, that depends on who we're dealing with, what their top clearance is, and whether this was a long-term Soviet infiltration operation, or whether it's just someone who got themselves backed into a corner. Maybe this person is loyal to the Soviets, or then again, maybe they're being blackmailed or got in some financial trouble. The first thing we'd do is set up surveillance, try to figure out how deep it goes, and whether it would be worth feeding this person misinformation. If not, we have the FBI make an arrest for espionage against this country. You know the drill. It's not pretty. Either way, your friend is in for a rough time." Colby looked at Abbott. "Chin up, you just got yourself a new security clearance."

Abbott shivered in the wet morning air. "What makes a person decide to do something like this?"

Colby stood up and stretched a bit. "Money or politics. That's what it always comes down to, isn't it? Come on, let's go call the Secretary."

* * * * *

"Go home, Max," Shulmel Berglass told Max Rudger in Mossad headquarters, Tel Aviv. "Go back to your farm in Switzerland. Your job is over. You were a great success."

"I know you'll be sendin' commandos in there with the Yanks as soon as you get the word. I know the Israelis want to be part of this operation. Let me be a part of it too. I'll do you good. I could be an asset in an operation like this."

Shulmel Berglass sat down and looked at Max. "These men know their job. They would not need your assistance. You would only be in the way, I'm afraid."

"Bullshit. I can take orders as well as anyone. And I'm trained just as well." Max leaned his big arms on Berglass's desk and locked his hands together. ". . . Listen, old son, I have a debt to pay. Madison could be in that camp alone right now because I got a blasted case of cold feet at the last minute. You've got to let me go."

Berglass spoke gently, not wanting to look into Max's eyes as he explained, "I am sorry, my friend, truly sorry, but it is impossible. Our commandos are young and strong, as they must be in order to be effective. You've done very well, but you are too old now for combat. Please do not make me say more. Go now. Israel has paid you very well for your trouble. I have issued instructions to my assistants to see that you are on the next plane to Zurich. They are prepared to use force if necessary." He stood and held out his hand. "Goodbye, Max, and thank you again."

Max Rudger turned slowly without saying goodbye, and followed his armed escorts out of the building to a waiting automobile.

Shulmel Berglass sat back down at his desk and sighed sadly. It was not the first time he had had to dismiss someone who didn't know his limits, someone with the heart and mind to serve. It was never a pleasant job, and he wondered vaguely when he himself might be the recipient of such an order.

* * * * *

Flanked by the snow-capped peaks of Mt. Hermon, the southern end of the rich Bekaa Valley was littered with aluminum buildings of assorted shapes and sizes. Two major training camps, within a mile of each other, occupied this particular section of the Bekaa.

Providence's camps, the largest in the valley, boasted twelve buildings, a training staff of twenty, a maintenance and domestic staff of ten, and were able to train up to one hundred recruits at any one time. The area immediately surrounding the "huts" was protected by eight feet of barbed wire. Beyond the wire and between the base of the Anti-Lebanon

Mountains and the huts, was a large meadow used for outdoor training exercises between satellite passes. The exposed and more accessible sides of the camp were secured by the random placement of booby traps, and the one dirt road leading to the camp gates was heavily patrolled. Madison was warned not to venture beyond the camp borders without an escort. After all, the training staff at this camp was very safety conscious, she was told, and the pure irony in that simple statement had nearly made her laugh aloud.

The meal that evening was simple, roast lamb, black bread, beans and potatoes. The conversation was loud and bright. Twenty trainers, joined by Ahmed Tahril, Madison McGuire and Yael Chazan, gathered in the camp cafeteria for their last private meal before the next day's influx of new recruits. Madison was introduced simply as Madison, an observer and former Intelligence officer.

Michael Peelor, who had taken a seat next to her, whispered, "Everything is strictly first names here. No background data. These guys are here to do a job, to train. They don't want to get involved with us, with each other or with the operation as a whole. Talking about anything we do outside the camp is strictly taboo. It's for everyone's protection."

After the meal, Abu Khaled, a tall, dark Palestinian whose name Madison had heard connected with terror around the world, gave Madison a tour of the camp. Five of the buildings, he told her in perfect English, were barracks reserved for the male trainers and recruits. One building housed female guests, one nearly the size of a gymnasium was used for demonstrations and training, another stored weapons and ammunition, and one protected automobiles and large equipment from the eyes of U.S. satellites.

"And what about the other three?" Madison asked, standing next to Khaled in the front of the semicircle of buildings.

"Hut number one is Ahmed's private quarters. You are invited to join us there later."

Madison looked at buildings number two and twelve, the buildings that Khaled had deliberately ignored, the only two with armed guards pacing out front. She wanted to ask what secrets they housed, but Khaled's black eyes, glistening in the half darkness of the camp, warned her off.

Inside Ahmed Tahril's private quarters, tall mugs of dark tea were passed out. Tahril toasted Khaled's continued loyalty and effectiveness, Michael and Yael's part in the embassy bombing, and Madison's brave efforts in "neutralizing" the Israeli spy. He praised all of them generously, his smooth voice even, his round brown eyes soft and sincere. Madison knew, as she watched the beaming, honored faces of the group, that Ahmed Tahril was casting his spell on them, pulling them further into his world.

With the absolution and appreciation of their leader fresh in their minds, and hot tea in their stomachs, Michael and Abu disappeared into the trainers' hut, and Madison and Yael retired to hut number seven.

Barely an hour later, after their conversation had trailed off, as Madison lay in one of the twenty-four bunk beds planning how she would expose the camp, she heard Yael withdraw quietly from the bed next to hers and slip out of the building.

Madison eased her way silently out the door and moved along the side of the huts, skillfully shadowing Yael at twenty yards. She watched Yael tap on Tahril's door, watched in utter astonishment as his fleshy arms wrapped around her small waist and pulled her to him, watched the door close and the inside lights go out.

She made her way back to hut number seven and sat down on the dry ground outside, leaning against the building and lighting a cigarette. At twelve-thirty she noted the changing of the guards outside hut number two. The sturdy antennas on the roof and blue-white glow from under the door told her this was the building that housed the communications equipment, the building she must penetrate in order to reach her contact and relay her location, for there appeared to be no other communication equipment of any kind in all the other huts she had seen. No telephones, no facsimile machines, no computers.

Tahril's door opened, and then closed just as quickly. Madison saw Yael's dark figure coming towards her in the dim light. Yael's pace slowed as she saw Madison sitting outside.

"Lovely evening, isn't it?" Madison asked casually.

Yael sat down next to her. "No one knows, Madison."

Madison spoke without judgment or analysis, quelling Yael's concerns without being asked. "Your secret is quite safe."

"I love him," Yael announced with a trace of sadness in her voice.

"And does he love you?" Madison inquired softly, not looking at her.

"Yes, in his way," was the reply after some thought. "But Ahmed is a very busy man, an important man. He has the camp, he has our people and he has two wives already."

Madison sat outside for another thirty minutes after Yael had gone in. She looked at Tahril's hut, and whispered, "You bastard."

* * * * *

My Lord, they're just children, Madison reflected grimly as a busload of sixty new recruits arrived in the camp. Yael explained that most of them came from the flea and lice infested camps of the Occupied Territory.

The recruits were herded like frightened sheep to their quarters and ordered to turn over their clothing and to climb into the showers. They were given special shampoo and soaps with fungicides. Their clothes were destroyed and replaced by light-weight khaki uniforms furnished by the Libyan government. Their diets would be controlled and kept relatively bland for the first two weeks while their systems slowly adjusted to adequate portions of healthy foods.

All of them were thin and gaunt, and Madison's heart spasmed when she walked into the women's barracks and found eleven naked, hollow-cheeked young women standing in a line, as they had been instructed, waiting for their uniforms, silent and uncomplaining.

Their eyes probed her as she stood in front of them in her jeans and T-shirt and expensive running shoes, searching for something comforting to say. "I'm afraid I don't speak Arabic," she announced first in English, then in German and French.

"Some English here," answered a striking young woman with dark hair and green-blue eyes, who stood with her arms folded timidly over her bare breasts. "I am Yursha."

"My name is Madison. I'll see about your clothes." No one answered, but Madison smiled at the roar of conversation that erupted behind her when she stepped outside.

Two male trainers were coming towards the hut with uniforms in their arms as Madison stepped out. "Thank you. I'll carry them inside."

One of the trainers, an Englishman named Edward who she had met the night before at dinner, smiled as he dropped the load of clothing into her arms. "Seen it all before, love," he said, giving a wink.

Madison smiled brightly. "Good then, you won't be missing anything."

* * * * *

It was "the Farm" all over again. It was the next batch of CIA operatives and all their good intentions. It was rows of fresh new recruits lining up and marching to sit in metal chairs for their initial indoctrination. It was a group of baby faces waiting to hear the Director speak of loyalty and dedication and the importance of serving one's country. It was young Madison McGuire, daughter of dead hero Jake McGuire, sitting there in the front row of her great calling, soaking in every word the Director uttered and secretly believing that those words were designed for her ears only. And it was young Madison who would emerge from that tidy group with a fire inside her, convinced that she could help save the world from itself. It was Madison, the future spy, betrayer and killer, who would naively and egotistically carry the burden of this belief with her for the next half of her life.

Madison had drifted back twenty years in the last five minutes of watching the freshly showered, uniformed recruits find their places in building number eight. There was an excitement in the air that had taken her back — a spark coming from inside them that could not be extinguished. But on this day Ahmed Tahril was its owner and tempter, its master and prompter.

Tahril strode across the platform and a mortuary-like quiet settled over the building as every set of eyes fixed on him and every set of ears anticipated the tones of his great voice and its words of inspiration. He paused and looked out onto his audience, his soft, needy eyes sweeping over them; and at that moment Madison was sure that Ahmed Tahril had never made a small or unimpressive entrance in his life.

He spoke to them in their own language, in the voice of a leader, then a father, then a friend. And though Madison could not understand his words, the resonant, adulatory tones made his meaning quite clear. You are the chosen ones, he was telling them, while their grateful eyes followed him around the platform. You are the liberators, the bold warriors who fight for Palestine.

Madison looked over the audience at the clouded, hypnotized stares and the eyes turned upward to their leader, their one accessible shining star, their promise. Repelled, she turned away and slipped through the door.

* * * * *

Terry Woodall, sitting on the couch with a T.V. dinner in her lap, laughed to herself about the telephone conversation she had had with Marge Price when Marge had suggested that Terry make more friends, go out, or find a support group. Terry wondered absently if she could find a support group in Buxton, North Carolina, which focused on the issues surrounding lesbians whose lovers were CIA agents. And if such a group existed, she thought half amused, what would they call themselves? Perhaps L.O.I.S. for Lovers Of Insensitive Spies. Or Spookanon, Alaspy or S.S.O.P.T.S.H.W&W (Same Sex Operatives Partners That Sit Home Worrying and Waiting). Maybe even Combat Wives Anonymous . . . The possibilities were endless and quite intriguing.

The telephone rang and she bolted to catch it before the answering machine. The voice on the other end was a welcome friend.

"Terry, you gorgeous hunk of woman. How have you been keepin' yourself?"

"Max Rudger, we haven't heard from you since Christmas." She sat back down on the couch, conscious that she had used we instead of I as she had out of habit many times in the last weeks.

"Been here and there. Germany, the Middle East for a bit. You have a world traveler on the line, old girl."

Terry smiled. "I'm impressed."

"Easily impressed, aren't you now? I suppose Madi McGuire's evidence enough of that." Terry laughed, and Max continued. "Saw the old battle-axe, by the way. She says to tell you she's safe," Max reported, and then added his own interpretation. "Says she's been a real dumb shit and she misses you."

"Thank God she's all right," Terry said quietly. "How is she, really, Max? How does she look? I saw some footage on television. She was —"

"Yeah, I know. That's kind of how I found her. She always has been a headline grabber. Not hard to find if you know where to look. And she looks fine." He paused. "Never seems to age like the rest of us."

"Do you know when she's coming home?"

"Don't know much about what she's doing," Max lied, "but my guess is you'll be seeing her soon. Now then, does that make you happy?"

"Yes, very happy."

"Good. Wanted you to be primed before I gave you the news. I'm getting married next month. Can you believe it? It would mean a lot if you both could come."

"You couldn't keep us away. Congratulations."

"Well then, have the old bag call me when she gets home . . . And Terry, don't you be worryin' none about her. She's got a good head on those shoulders of hers. I know she'll be just fine," Max lied again, this time as much for his own peace of mind as for Terry's.

* * * * *

Terry found paper and pen and started a letter to Madison:

I've been in Washington, Madison, and I have imagined that I could trace your footsteps through its streets and feel those mysterious feelings you have for the city. I've studied its secret agencies from afar. I've looked at the buildings and the people that always seemed so ugly to me, and I've tried to see them through your eyes. And I think I know now why you find it so beautiful. It's the promise that you will not have to follow a life that hasn't been lived by you before.

I've relived the day that you first kissed me, and made love to me, and then silently planned your escape while you thought I was sleeping. I remember the fear in your eyes when you came back to our bed, realizing that you loved me and you could not make yourself leave . . . Why you are so terrified to love and be loved is something that is just beginning to be clear to me.

And when you come home, we can sit on our little strip of beach and talk it out. We can take walks at dusk and watch the tide roll in. We can laugh at Stray Cat who misses you terribly, and if you would like, my love, we can peer through keyholes at the setting sun.

Terry folded the letter neatly into an envelope, scribbled Madison's name across the front and set it on the kitchen table.

"You are my hope," she whispered to the envelope, as Stray Cat rubbed against her legs contentedly.

* * * * *

It was Friday. The porch light had been left burning and Katherine Maloane was on time for the first show at the Comedy Club for the second week in a row. And for the second consecutive week she had walked those last four blocks to her State Department office, and for the second week she had searched in vain for the orange chalk mark that told her her message had been received.

Why were they not responding? Last week's note had told them clearly that she had not been detected as they had wrongly suspected. Her security clearance had remained the same, although still far from top level. She had not been questioned, had not been treated differently and she had not been followed, as far as she knew.

Tonight she had decided to break the rules. Tonight she would leave something under the ashtray and wait to see who stepped out of the shadows to gather the information. Tonight she would approach the courier and demand to see her controller, Nikolai Mikhailovich Orstroklova.

She waited nervously for the first show to end. She ordered three drinks and finished two. She laughed when the others laughed, although she had not heard one joke. She picked at her fingernails and adjusted herself in her seat. She looked at the faces around her in desperation and hated them for their comfort. She slipped her hand inside her shoulder bag and felt for the handle of the .22 caliber pistol. Tonight she would make her demands and tonight, she thought as she released the safety, they would listen.

The first show was reaching its peak. The laughter was growing louder, the language on stage becoming more and more obscene, which seemed to greatly please audiences these days, Katherine noted absently as she slipped a folded note under the ashtray and rose from her seat.

In the restroom, she performed for the mirror, straightening a stray lock of blonde hair here and there and checking the whiteness of her teeth, until she believed the room had emptied. Her heart pounding, she peeked out to see who might be removing the note from her table. What would she say, she wondered as she planned her approach. I am Bluebird and I demand to see Nikolai? I am Bluebird and I have a gun? She reached in her bag once again and cupped her hand around the tiny revolver. It was then that she heard the creak of a stall door behind her and felt the sharp jab in her ribs.

"Step into a stall, please, and turn over your weapon," was the quiet order.

"Where is Yuri Vissarinovich, Bluebird?" a small, hard woman insisted once they were safely locked away. "Where is he kept safe?"

Katherine looked at the woman, stunned. "I don't know anyone named Yuri. Where is Nikolai? I demand to speak to my controller."

The bathroom door opened and closed. A stall door opened and closed and locked. The Soviet agent pressed the blue steel of her weapon into Katherine's neck, warning her not to speak. They waited there through the sounds of someone relieving herself, waited through the washing of the hands and the brushing of the hair, waited until the door opened and closed again, and then waited another few seconds for good measure.

"You passed information about an agent, code name Scorpion. What did it mean?" the woman demanded after a lifetime of silence.

"What do you mean, what did it mean?" Katherine answered, her panic mounting, her mind searching for a way out. "It meant Scorpion was being flown to Frankfurt to —"

"Scorpion never arrived in Frankfurt, was never detected," the woman hissed from inches below her ear. "Yuri made his report and then he disappeared. It was a signal, was it not? A code telling him he could defect?"

Katherine wanted to look at the woman, wanted to find her eyes and convince them that she was telling the truth, but the gun was pressing harder into her thin neck, making it impossible to move.

"*Defect* . . . I don't know anything about that," she answered stiffly, her back pressed against the metal door. "Nikolai doesn't tell me anything about what you people do."

The outside door opened again and two quiet knocks were heard against the stall door.

"She refuses to cooperate. She had a weapon," the woman told a larger woman agent who pushed her way into the crowded cubicle.

The next few seconds seemed strangely out of time with the rest of the world. There was excruciating pain. There was the larger woman's big hands pinching a nerve in her shoulder near her neck and covering her mouth. There was a cold gouge near her left elbow and then a rush of heat. There was the background noise that her mind seemed to want to grab onto, music, glasses rattling and laughter. And then there was the sound of her own breathing becoming louder and louder and the vague feeling of the floor giving way as her body hit it.

Thomas Wright checked his watch and looked at the restroom door once again. Five women had exited that room in the last seven minutes since Katherine Maloane, the subject of his surveillance, had disappeared inside. He reached for the arm of a passing waitress and explained apologetically, as he handed over a ten dollar bill, that his date wasn't feeling well and asked if she would mind checking the restroom to be sure everything was okay.

Moments later a crowd was gathering outside the door, the bartender was calling an ambulance and Thomas Wright was on the line to Langley.

CHAPTER FIFTEEN

"There's your answer, Greg," Mitchell Colby growled as he passed the printed report across the desk. "We found four grams in her condo. The fingerprints on the bag and a cut-off straw matched hers. She was a user. Probably needed the money to support her habit. She must have just done too much last night. How in the hell does someone like that manage to maintain a position at State?"

Greg Abbott had found a small stain on the carpet just inches from his feet and was staring at it purposefully. "But there was no sign she had ever used a needle before, right? No old marks, nothing but a perforated septum, and all that indicates is she had just been sniffing for a while, not shooting it." He looked up slowly from the carpet. "Why would she decide to start last night? And why wasn't anything found on her body? No drugs, no syringe. Nothing."

Colby leaned forward gently. "I know she was a friend. But remember, Katherine Maloane was also a traitor . . . a Soviet puppet. Let it go, son. It's not worth it."

Abbott pushed himself out of his chair and looked at the Director. "Not *worth* it? We're talking about a human life here, and you know as well as I do that this was a murder and it should be treated as such," he blurted, hearing his own voice and knowing immediately that it was too loud. And as he feared, the wrath of Mitchell Colby, the Director of Central Intelligence, the guardian of state secrets, was thrust upon him.

"Sit *down* and listen to me. First of all there is no proof whatsoever to indicate foul play," he said in his most intimidating manner while counting off each point on his stubby fingers. "And secondly, think about what's at stake here. Do you want to take responsibility for what could happen if we accused Soviet agents of killing one of our people? We're talking about more than the Cold War here, boy, we're talking about possible *overt military action*. Do you know what that means in this day and age? Why, it's unspeakable." He sighed and leaned back and then lowered his big voice to a calmness Abbott found chilling. "Now, go somewhere and think this thing out until you're rational again."

* * * * *

It was more of a military academy than a terrorist camp. The focus was on discipline, the regimen strict and controlled. Before dawn the group was fed in the cafeteria then taken outside at sunrise for weapons and explosives training. Mid-morning saw them being rushed inside while the first U.S. satellite of the day made its pass over a benign scene.

The recruits were in what Michael Peelor called the two-week assessment period, during which the troops were run through a shortened version of the complete training course and evaluated for special strengths or weaknesses. When the assessment period was over, the team would be divided into small groups and placed in different courses depending on their talents. Each course and each group was considered equally important to the ultimate goal. Some of the young people would be placed in the destabilization course, which taught crowd incitement and propaganda campaigns. Others would learn evasion techniques, weapons handling, and vehicle-based assaults such as abductions and hostage taking.

The training was grueling for these new recruits, and for the last three days Madison had watched them exercising and running and shrieking with their weapons in their hands. For the last three evenings she had watched them study the manuals they were given detailing the principles of sabotage and guerrilla warfare, and then she had seen them crawl into their bunks and fall asleep, exhausted.

One evening when Madison had taken her

213

nightly post outside the hut, where she smoked cigarettes and watched the guards changing at hut numbers two and twelve, she heard the door open behind her and felt a brush at her sleeve. The young woman named Yursha had joined her, not unexpectedly. For Madison had noticed Yursha watching her curiously in the last few days.

She had watched Yursha change since she had arrived in the camp, watched her imitate Madison's walk and movements, watched her take on a new air of confidence, watched her learn weapons handling quickly, and rise to the head of her group.

"It's Yursha, isn't it?" Madison asked, after Yursha did not speak.

"Yes," answered the young woman with the striking light eyes.

"Can't you sleep? You should be quite exhausted."

"I want to see what brings you here each night," she answered, obviously shy about her English, looking at the ground.

Madison held up her cigarette. "Never smoke in bed. It's very dangerous."

Yursha looked at her and smiled. "Ah, I think it is more. You are . . . ah . . . restless. I see you run before the sun as we go to breakfast. Yael tells us you love to run. I say you hate to be still. There is a difference."

A smile slowly formed on Madison's face. Yursha lowered her eyes, a bit embarrassed by her bold observation. "A valid assessment, I must say. You're quite right, I'm feeling a bit trapped. How about you?"

Yursha shook her head. "No, not trapped. Very happy. Trapped before. Now I am free."

Madison considered this for a moment. "Is that why you've come here, Yursha? For your freedom?"

Yursha looked across the camp. "Yes. The others say they come here for learn secrets they can take back with them, secrets that will help free our people. I am here because I never want go back to Rafah Camp, because I do not want to marry and have daughters. In Israel the Palestinian is oppressed. But in Palestine the men are our oppressors. Which is the better? In Gaza I have the beatings of my father and seven brothers. They want me to marry so I can be beat by a husband and they will no longer have to share food with me. Here is equality for women. Here women can be what they want."

"Is this really what you want to be, Yursha?"

Yursha nodded. "Want be free, yes."

"What happens when you leave here? Where will you go?"

"I have been promised schooling and support. Ahmed Tahril himself came speak with me. He said I am very bright, learning very fast. I will live in Germany until I am called."

"Called?"

"Until I am called to repay my debt," Yursha answered impatiently, as if Madison should already understand this.

"And if you don't survive that calling?"

Yursha turned and faced Madison. "It is risk I must take. It is the only way out for me."

Madison was suddenly so overcome by the sheer helplessness of the situation that she felt her eyes filling uncontrollably.

Yursha touched her hand. "Do not cry for me. It

is the others, it is the women of the camps who deserve our tears."

* * * * *

In building number eight, the first demonstration was being carried out by six of the trainers while Ahmed Tahril and the recruits looked on. An automobile had been driven into the building and a mock roadside hit squad had prepared a roadblock. The objective was to assassinate the passenger in the back seat, said to be an enemy of the cause. The group of mercenaries went through the simulation several times, each time with a new scenario, stopping to explain to the recruits what mistakes were made, what unexpected problems might occur and how to deal with the problems.

Madison, standing against the wall to the side of the demonstration, gradually made her way to the door. Time to move, she told herself, time to reach the communications hut, hopefully without blowing her cover, although she realized that this was a very real possibility. After days of collecting Intelligence, days of spying, she now knew which guard would be standing in front of hut number two and his name. She had made a point to chat with all the guards and trainers and find out as much as possible about each one. Sean, a young Irish soldier of fortune, would be guarding the communications hut today. They had spoken on her first night there and he had been delighted when she recognized his accent and volunteered that her grandfather and father had both been born near Dublin.

216

She slipped out the door and moved purposefully towards him, trying to catch his eye. She had crossed nearly half the camp before he noticed her and smiled.

She said, "They want you inside, love, to watch the games. Seems someone thinks you deserve a break. I'll stay here if you'd like. I could use a bit of fresh air anyway."

Sean rested the butt of his AK-47 against the ground and leaned the barrel against his leg. "Well now, that's what I like to hear."

Madison smiled and waved him away. "Go on then, I'll be right here."

She watched him walk into building number eight before she turned and began picking the lock on the communications hut.

The small hut was cluttered with used government equipment, radios, a computer terminal on an old desk, cables and wires tangled and stretched across the floor. Madison searched the files, trying to find something that listed the exact location of the camp, longitude and latitude. There was nothing. She picked up the handset on the PRC-77 transceiver, a green lunch-box sized radio, and turned the channel selector to the proper frequency, 40.93. She used the call-sign Abbott had given her in Beirut. "Libra Two, this is Eagle One, over." She repeated the transmission twice before the radio operator responded amidst a flood of static.

"Eagle One, this is Libra Two. Go ahead."

"Libra Two, I need a phone patch to Patriot one-nine-zero. I authenticate with code Babylon, over."

"Eagle One authenticated with code Babylon," was the response. "Phone patch to Patriot one-nine-zero now complete. Go ahead."

Madison smiled. She was now patched into the CIA's senior Intelligence officer in Beirut. She began. "Patriot this is Eagle One, over."

"Eagle One this is Patriot. You're breaking up. Relay location at once."

The crackling was louder, the Intelligence officer's words barely audible. Madison answered hurriedly. "Location is extreme southern tip of the Bekaa Valley, near the Syrian border, over."

There was no response. Madison repeated the transmission and again there was no response. "Damn," she muttered, and then, knowing that her one chance at the equipment had failed, she jerked wires and cables loose from the equipment and crashed the radio into the computer terminal, making sure that no one else would have use of the equipment.

Inside number eight, Michael Peelor turned away from the demonstration and saw Sean leaning against the wall.

"Madison's keepin' an eye on number two," Sean volunteered when Peelor approached.

Madison had just locked the door and posted herself outside the hut when she saw Michael Peelor come out of building eight. Her mind was racing, questioning. Had the senior officer in Beirut received her transmission? She must operate on the assumption that he had not. How would she get the message to her agency now?

Peelor stopped in front of her and frowned. "What's going on?" he inquired suspiciously.

Madison shrugged casually. "Sean needed a break. Is there a problem?"

Peelor reached behind her and checked the hut door to be sure it was secure. "You tell me, Madison. Do we have a problem?"

They looked at one another for several seconds, Peelor's grey eyes searching hers, Madison staring back at him.

She smiled. "No problem I can see, old man. All is quiet in the camp."

"I'll take over," Peelor said without returning her smile, and then watched her uncertainly as she walked away.

*　*　*　*　*

He stalked the tiled corridors of Central Intelligence headquarters in Langley, Virginia, the closed doors on each side flitting past him like freeway traffic.

The voice stress and analysis test had just come through and verified that the partial transmission received in Beirut less than an hour ago was indeed the voice of the operative Madison McGuire. But Greg Abbott had told them that already, just as he had told them the substance of the sentence which had been interrupted when communications broke down.

"She said she was in the southern tip, when we lost voice contact. She was about to say that the target site is located in the southern tip of the Bekaa Valley," he had insisted, but the powers-that-be had dismissed him from the emergency meeting, saying that they needed something more concrete.

He had tried using simple logic by reminding them that camp number four-fifty-six, the camp to which he had paid particular attention in the last few days, was not only showing more activity on infrared photos, but was also located in the southern end of the Valley.

Fred Nolan, Deputy Director of Intelligence, had come to his defense on this point, telling those present of reports received from Israeli reconnaissance aircraft showing increased activity at the same camp. But he had quickly added that it was not unusual for the camps to be at full capacity this time of year, as spring and summer seemed to be the preferred training times for terrorist organizations.

They had all managed to agree, however, that the Delta team now on call in Cyprus should be alerted and its readiness increased. This was the most Greg Abbott was able to secure, considering his lack of "concrete" evidence. He also convinced Colby to allow him to work with a group of analysts whose primary focus would be camp number four-fifty-six.

He walked the halls deliberately, his frustration and exhaustion giving way to a lucidity and clarity he had not felt since the murder of Katherine Maloane. He was sure it was camp number four-fifty-six they wanted. Something inside him had made him absolutely inflexible on this point, something more than instinct, something deeper that had risen to the surface and given him this undeniable perception. Unfortunately it was something he was unable to explain to the others, and when he had tried, Mitchell Colby had interrupted and reminded him that the CIA dealt in Intelligence and was not an organization interested in parapsychology.

* * * * *

The instructors were blowing the whistles that hung around their necks. A roar of automobile engines, the clanking of equipment and the slamming of doors could be heard across the camp.

"Fifteen minutes, fifteen minutes," they were shouting, as the occupants of the camp carried out their rehearsed duties and scrambled to get to their huts before the dreaded afternoon satellite pass.

Madison had joined the women in their hut when the whistles sounded. She sat on her bunk, legs crossed in a yoga position, and pulled off the white scarf she wore to protect her from the thick dust that clouded the camp during the outside exercises. She twisted the scarf absently around one hand, while listening to the chatter around her, then folded it into a neat square. It was then that the idea struck her.

She checked her watch. Five minutes before the satellite pass. Her eyes swept over the room and found a broom leaning against the wall. Looking at the young women, she noticed to her relief that Yael was absent. The countdown began. Three more minutes, now two, now one . . . She rose calmly and tied her scarf around the broom handle, took a deep breath and cracked the door cautiously. The camp had been deserted. It's a ghost town in an old western, Madison thought, in one of those annoying moments when the mind wanders away from its immediate objectives.

She took a step outside and closed the door gently so as not to attract the attention of the would-be terrorists inside.

Yursha jerked open the door. "Madison, you are not allowed outside."

Madison did not look back, she did not want to see Yursha's questioning eyes. Instead she hoisted the broom with its white flag and walked directly to the center of the camp where she stood perfectly still in hopes that the passing satellite would send the picture back to the United States.

Inside hut number three, Abu Khaled sat on one of the bunks, Michael Peelor stretched out on another, and the rest of the trainers were in various stages of relaxation, taking advantage of the break. Khaled, who, according to Michael, found relaxation a bizarre concept, checked the time impatiently and began to pace, as he always did when they were confined to quarters.

Peelor looked at one of the older trainers, an Iraqi named Fouad, and smiled. "In ten seconds he'll walk to the door, open it, sigh, and then slam it." He yelled to Khaled, "Give yourself a break, Abu."

Khaled seemed to mutter something and then went to the door as predicted. Michael and Fouad exchanged smiles. Suddenly Abu Khaled drew his pistol and began shouting in Arabic. "The woman . . . the woman . . . she is sending a signal."

Michael Peelor was at his side in seconds. He

grabbed Khaled's shoulder and spun him around as Khaled was stomping out the door. "No shooting, Abu. Ahmed will want to deal with this."

Khaled's black eyes flashed his bitterness as he pulled away from Michael and ran towards Madison.

She saw him coming, saw Michael running behind him, but it was too late. To run would have invited his bullets. She stood there, her heart racing, clenching her jaw in anticipation, still holding the broom in the air, the white scarf blowing in the breeze.

Khaled jerked the broom from her hand and broke it over his knee, trembling in his rage. He moved very close to her and placed the pistol against her neck. "You will die for this."

An oily mist glistened on his face, forming tiny beads on his upper lip. The smell of his breath reminded Madison of stale wine and onion soup. His eyes, sunken and self-obsessed, bore into her. She held his stare, knowing it might be her last act of defiance.

Khaled's shouting had shaken the camp, and one by one hut doors were opening. Peelor was yelling to the others, "Stay inside, stay inside. The satellite is still in range."

In Tahril's private quarters, he paced around her in a circle, occasionally stopping to look at her as he decided her fate. Abu Khaled held her arms twisted up painfully behind her. Michael and Yael stood silently watching.

"You have made a great error, Madison, and now you have been exposed," Tahril told her calmly. "You were very convincing. We all believed this charade. Tell me, do you hate the Palestinian people so much that you would sabotage their hopes and dreams? Do you love the Jews so much that you —"

"No," Madison broke in, yanking her arms free from Khaled's grip. "I hate what they're doing to you and I hate what you're doing to them. Can't you see that killing innocent civilians is not the answer to your problems or the dream of your people?"

Tahril stood in front of her, arms linked across his chest. "There is no such thing as an innocent civilian in war. You should know this. There is only one rule in war and that is winning." He pointed one round finger at his own chest and snarled. "I am the voice of the Palestinian. I know what is right for my people."

"The people, Ahmed, have chosen their voice. And whether you think them too moderate or I think them too radical, there is only one appointed representative of the Palestinian people, and it's not you or your group of killers."

"You dare to speak of the P.L.O. in my camp?" he roared. "I spit on the P.L.O. and their moderate pandering. The P.L.O. betrays and belittles my people with their silly pleas to negotiate. There is only one way to peace in this world. Israel must be destroyed."

She was out of control now, and she knew it. But the weeks of frustration had crept up on her.

She placed her hands on her hips and laughed at him, which drew a gasp from Yael Chazan. "Ahmed Tahril, the great self-appointed spokesman. Ahmed Tahril, who kills his own if they don't subscribe to his views. Ahmed Tahril, the pretender. It is you who belittles the Palestinian. Do you think they want the world to look at them as killers? Do you think they want to be thought of as terrorists?" She leaned closer to his face, taunting him. "Get out of the *bloody* way, Ahmed, and give them a chance to have their peace."

Tahril's door was flung open by one of his operatives who reported, "The communications equipment has been sabotaged. It is no longer operational."

Madison saw it coming, saw the rage in his face, saw the flat of his hand moving closer. She braced herself just as the stinging blow hit her. But before the trickle of blood from her lip had made it to her chin, she went into action. Her right foot slammed into Tahril's crotch. Her elbow crashed into Khaled's abdomen. She was poised to administer another blow to Khaled when Michael Peelor fired his pistol into the floorboards between her feet.

Tahril, furious and doubled up on the floor, managed to croak, "Take her to number twelve, Abu. Tomorrow when the light is good we will film the hanging and show the Americans what we do with their spies."

CHAPTER SIXTEEN

The bewildered guard stepped aside as Abu
Khaled hurled Madison into building number twelve.
She picked herself up and turned to investigate the
one building in the camp she had not been able to
penetrate.

She gasped when she saw his dull eyes peering
at her through the greasy hair that had fallen onto
his forehead. And then, she recognized the man from
the photographs that appeared in the paper and on
television on those rare occasions when America
allowed itself to remember its hostages.

His name was Frank Rice. It had been last August when she had seen the former Beirut University college professor on a video tape that his captors had filmed. It was his fifty-second birthday, the anchorman had told the country solemnly, and it marked his thirty-sixth month in captivity.

From what Madison remembered of him, his sharp, thin face, his slight build, it hardly seemed possible that they could have taken much of anything from him physically. But they had taken a good twenty pounds more, and it had come from all over him, his wrists, his face and arms. They had taken his dark hair and given him shocking streaks of white. They had made his fine straight nose crooked with their beatings. And they had taken his dignity, by putting him on a four-foot chain and attaching it to the radiator, releasing him once a day, she later discovered, to go to the toilet.

Sickened, she moved towards the compliant, crouching shell of a man and squatted next to him. He had the dungeon paleness of a long-term prisoner, and his glazed eyes looked out at her submissively as if she were just another one of his interrogators.

"My name is Madison McGuire, Mr. Rice," she said softly, touching his thin wrist. "I recognize you from American television. I'm with the CIA. We're going to take you home very soon, sir." And then in a whisper, to frustrate any listening devices that might be planted there, she spoke into his right ear. "I was caught sending a signal home. I completed that signal. It should only be a matter of hours now," she said, as frightened as she had ever been in her life and hoping to God it was true.

He looked at her for a moment as if he could not comprehend the meaning of her words. She smiled and nodded. "You'll be home soon," she reassured him again. His dark eyes showed a spark of life and then filled with tears and he fell into her and began to sob, his frail body convulsing in her arms.

She held him for what seemed like hours. She rocked him and assured him and stroked his dirty hair. She brought him water from a sink in the corner that his jailers, in their cruelty, had put just out of his reach, and he drank it from her cupped hands because they had provided no cup or glass.

She helped him to his feet and forced him to walk back and forth on his short chain, telling him he must exercise his muscles in case he had to run to escape. She searched the room for a way out, and tugged in vain at his chain to free him. She heard Greg Abbott's voice telling her that they could have reinforcements there within an hour of her signal. She paced and sat, and then paced and sat again, and wondered how this man had endured more than three years in captivity.

* * * * *

In building number eight, the trainers were passing out weapons and Ahmed Tahril was telling the group that the first test of their loyalty might be coming. An American spy had infiltrated the organization, he told them from his elevated platform. But it would take at least a day, perhaps longer, he said, for them to mobilize and find a way to reach the camps.

* * * * *

Greg Allen Abbott sat in a fifth floor office with two CIA analysts, watching as they divided up the stack of satellite photographs that had just been delivered. It was mid-morning in Langley and the pile of empty Styrofoam cups scattered around the table was the only evidence of this morning's work. The satellite photos were certainly not producing any usable intelligence, and no other telephone calls had come through from his agent in the Middle East.

"You want this stack, Greg?" one of the analysts asked. "We'll switch off when we're done to be sure we haven't missed anything."

Abbott nodded and sighed as he pulled the stack closer for inspection. Then they switched stacks and began again.

The second analyst commented, "Didn't get all their people inside on these shots. Four-fifty-six camp is getting careless."

Abbott's tired head shot up. "Show me what you saw, Carl."

"When?" the analyst asked.

"When you said they didn't have their people inside, goddammit."

Carl shoved a stack in front of Abbott. "I think it's in this group."

Abbott went through the pictures hurriedly, tossing aside several before he saw a figure standing in the center of a fenced area on one of the photos. He looked at the next one and saw the same figure. They're holding something, he thought, what the hell is it? He went to the next one and saw three people this time, huddled together.

Abbott grabbed the magnifying glass. The photographs were grainy and a bit distorted, and he was still unable to tell if the person was male or female. But the flag, the white flag blowing just feet above their heads, was unmistakable. Greg Abbott hit the door running.

* * * * *

Mitchell Colby buzzed his assistant. "Get me an enlargement of photo number one thousand and two, camp number four-fifty-six, pronto. And get me Vice Admiral Koch on the line, code red, I repeat, code red." He looked up at Abbott. "This could be it, son. If that enlargement looks good it'll be all we need to move." He smiled and shook his head. "Damned ingenious, wasn't it? The white flag and all."

Abbott nodded. "Yes, incredible."

Colby's phone buzzed and he grabbed it quickly. Vice Admiral Koch, in charge of the Joint Special Operations Command, was on the line. "Ready your people, Admiral. I'll know in minutes if we've located the target."

A knock at Colby's door interrupted his conversation. "Hold please, Admiral. I may have the answer for you right now."

The enlargement was rushed in by an assistant and Colby and Abbott studied it briefly.

"That's her, sir. That's Madison. We've found her. Good God, someone's holding a gun to her head."

Colby picked up the phone again. "We've got the location. I'll have the information sent to your office immediately. By the way, from the look of things our asset may be in a hostage situation. We're counting on your team, Admiral. Good luck."

Colby looked at Greg Abbott. "Well, that's it. Now all we can do is wait it out."

"Nothing more? We just sit here and wait?" Abbott asked.

"This is the first time you've been involved with a Special Forces operation. That's the way it works. We step back now. The JSOC has complete control of all antiterrorist forces, Greg, and answers only to the Joint Chiefs, who answer to the Secretary of Defense, who answers to the President. We're out of it now. We've done our part." Colby smiled. "It's always a little anticlimactic at this point and nerve-wracking as hell. How about a drink to celebrate a job well done anyway?"

* * * * *

On the Mediterranean island of Cyprus, in the city of Nicosia, four long-range Black Hawk helicopters, the minimum deemed necessary to carry out the operation, were being fueled and readied. The copters had been modified for their mission with infrared guidance and night vision systems and refueling gear that allowed them to fly a thousand miles without a refueling stopover.

Two of the giant machines would carry the commando team and one would provide air cover and return with any hostages found in the camps. The fourth helicopter was filled with highly sophisticated, classified communications equipment and would carry a Signal Intelligence officer who would keep the

President and the Chairman of the Joint Chiefs advised of the operation's progress through the use of a communication device commonly referred to as SATCOM. This device, hooked up with military satellites, allowed radar-safe transcontinental communications.

The four pilots, a team of twenty-five Delta Force commandos and one Intelligence officer, grouped around the senior officer in charge of the operation, Major General Steve Lakes, a wiry veteran Air Force combat pilot with two hundred and eighty-five Southeast Asia missions under his belt.

"Okay, this is how it reads right now. The Israelis have pulled out on their offer for ground support. But we've worked out a deal where they'll run a sea-air rescue mission in case we get into trouble and one of us goes down. No American fingerprints on this one, guys, so you pilots are going to have to evade Syrian radar for a hundred and sixty miles, and it's imperative that you ground team people leave nothing behind." He pointed to a red circle on a map he had laid out on the ground. "This is our destination, code name Nightingale, just over the Syrian border. Thirty-three point thirty north, thirty-five nineteen east. We'll have approximately half a mile to go on foot. Watch your step. They've booby trapped the area, you can bet your ass on that. We've got to go in quiet, find our asset, liberate any hostages. And take out this sonofabitch," he said, showing them a photograph of Ahmed Tahril. "He's top priority."

Major General Lakes then produced a copy of Madison's I.D. badge and passed it around. "This is our asset. We do everything possible to get her out.

Issue her a weapon as soon as you make contact. She's checked out on everything. Anyone else carrying weapons either lays it down or gets taken out point blank, no questions."

He spread out four satellite photos around on the ground for the soldiers to see. "Memorize this layout. This is the target. Twelve buildings in all and Intelligence says maybe up to a hundred troops. Half of them probably aren't battle ready. It shouldn't be a problem."

He pointed to buildings two and twelve. "These two buildings are the only ones with sentries outside. We have to assume that one of these is for prisoners. From our entry point we'll hit this one first, then move immediately to the last one, unless we encounter resistance along the way. We'll have fifteen minutes, I repeat, fifteen minutes max to carry out the operation before the Syrians get word we're there. Pilots be ready to move as soon as we radio in. You'll have to pluck us out of there."

He took one last look at the group. "All right, let's move."

It was no simple task even for the most experienced pilot. The sky was a dark blue, the moon obscured by clouds. The four Black Hawk helicopters, painted desert brown for their mission, flew just ten feet above rough waters in an effort to evade Syrian radar. The sea spray and salt coated their windshields with a crusty film and reduced visibility to nearly impossible levels. The soldiers sat quietly in the rear of the first two helicopters contemplating their mission, each lost in his own thoughts.

In the fourth copter, the Intelligence officer had

already linked up with the satellite and was making his report. "White Flag underway, sir. Nightingale ETA approximately fifty minutes. No close encounters of the wrong kind so far."

The ground team trotted noiselessly down the side of the dirt road that led to the camp's gate, purposely avoiding the grassy, booby trapped areas. The first Providence patrol had already been "surgically removed." Major General Steve Lakes, along with one other commando, had come from behind, pulled the two guards from their jeep and silently neutralized them in a matter of seconds.

The second patrol was in sight now, posted barely one hundred yards from the gate. Tony Cane, one of the youngest members of the group, slipped on his military issue night vision goggles, attached a heavy silencer to his rifle and took careful aim, aided by an IRT 1000 infrared aiming light. Two quick cracks from his rifle saw the guards tumble from their post to the ground. He then repeated the process and took out another five guards posted just inside the fence. The team immediately advanced to within twenty feet of the gate. Three commandos broke off from the group and went to work with their wire cutters. Barely two minutes later, the highly skilled group began filing into the borders of the sleeping terrorist camp, where they split up without discussion into two groups, and began working their way behind the buildings, using their knives to neutralize another six guards posted around the fence. One team headed towards building two, the other towards building twelve.

Team number one silenced the guard outside building two without incident, and found a communications room that had apparently already been sabotaged. They then moved outside and split into three groups of four, each group moving towards a hut door, waiting for the signal.

Inside building twelve, Madison McGuire sat on the floor dozing, with her head propped against the wall. The sound outside the thin aluminum walls brought her awake immediately. It was a sound she had heard before, and she knew that whoever was out there had just killed the guard.

She went to Frank Rice, shook him awake and made him move as close to the radiator as possible for cover. "This could be our wake-up call, Mr. Rice," she whispered. "Don't move and don't make a peep."

She moved next to the door and pressed herself against the wall. The door rattled, and then the next sound was so sharp and so loud that it startled even her. The butt of a rifle split the door and a Delta Force commando crashed through. At the same moment deafening gunfire erupted throughout the camp.

Madison held up both hands when the commando spun around and faced her. "McGuire, Madison, three double-o-three, CIA," she blurted.

The bearded commando smiled and yelled to the others outside. "I've got our asset."

He tossed Madison his H&K MP5 submachine gun. "Been looking for you, McGuire, Madison, three double-o-three. Hope you're up for some action. How many we got here?"

"Twenty professionals and seventy fresh recruits with no experience and only the basics in weapons handling."

"Where's the stockpile, and what are we dealing with?" the soldier asked hurriedly.

"The center building. They've got Soviet made RPG-7 rocket launchers, grenades, surface-to-air missiles and AK-47's."

His sharp eyes scanned the room. "What do we have here?" he asked, seeing Frank Rice huddled close to the radiator.

"American hostage, Frank Rice."

The commando moved quickly to the hostage. "Hang on, Mr. Rice. We've come to take you home. Don't be alarmed, sir. I'm just going to get you out of that chain the easy way. Hold real still." He aimed for the chain, barely six inches from Rice's ankle and fired. The chain snapped.

He turned to Madison. "Where would we find Tahril?"

"First building, closest to the gate," she answered and then looked at Frank Rice. "Get in the corner, Mr. Rice and stay there. We'll be back for you."

Tony Cane, followed by Madison, rushed out of the building and found two Delta commandos waiting to provide cover. "Got one hostage inside. Good condition. The target should be in the first building."

Amidst the gunfire, Major General Steve Lakes zigzagged through the camp and reached them, winded. "We've taken all but one of the buildings now. Buildings two, six and ten were empty. Haven't located our target yet."

The trainers' hut was the only building still under fire, its door open, two trainers standing inside exchanging fire with the commandos. Madison caught a glimpse of Michael Peelor running past the door. Then there was a terrific blast. Peelor, to her astonishment, was tossing grenades towards the trainers' hut. Madison pointed at Peelor, and told Major General Steve Lakes, "That one's on our side."

The trainers were running out now, firing at anything that moved. Four Special Force commandos went down immediately.

Madison thought about what the General had said: *Two, six and ten are empty.* Building number ten housed the vehicles at night and during satellite passes. Hiding there would not be a difficult task for a creative man like Ahmed Tahril. She moved around behind the hut and worked her way towards the building. Pushing the door open, she stepped inside just in time to catch him opening the bay door.

"Hold it right there, Tahril. Hands up, like a good boy," she ordered, the submachine gun pointed at his back.

Tahril lifted his hands as instructed . . . Then a sound from behind one of the jeeps . . . Then a blast from Yael Chazan's Israeli-made Uzi forced Madison to the floor.

She crawled on her stomach towards a line of jeeps, seeing Yael's feet moving around the vehicles, hearing an engine start up and knowing Tahril was in one of the jeeps.

"Hear that, Yael?" she yelled. "He's leaving you here to die alone. That's how much he loves you. Come out now and you've got a chance."

She raised her head cautiously and looked over one of the vehicles, but Yael was waiting for her and opened fire. Madison ducked down, breathing heavily as the bullets skimmed the jeep just inches from her head. She moved and took cover behind one of the other jeeps, found a clearing, raised up and fired. The hard, short burst of the MP5 knocked Yael backwards, sending her weapon flying from her hands, leaving her twisted and lifeless on the concrete floor.

Madison did not pause. Running after Tahril, she hurled herself onto the back of the jeep as it roared away. Tahril saw her in the rearview mirror as she was pulling herself up inside the vehicle and slammed on the brakes, sending her tumbling over the side of the jeep. As the jeep roared away again, Madison made it to her feet, positioned the submachine gun and aimed for the back of his head. She fired.

The camp was quiet now. Two U.S. commandos came running. One went to the jeep and found Tahril.

"He's a goner. Good job, CIA." He grabbed his radio and instructed the helicopters, "White Flag complete. Target down. Now get us out of this hellhole."

The second commando then went to Tahril's body and yanked off the heavy gold chain that had hung around the leader's neck. He smiled and held it up. "A souvenir," he announced proudly.

Disgusted, Madison tossed her weapon away and took one last pensive walk through the camp. She saw Michael Peelor lying dead on the ground, apparently killed by one of the terrorists he had turned on. His loyalty to his country had prevailed after all. As she pushed the blond hair off his face and pressed his eyelids closed, she told herself it was the way Peelor would have wanted to die. She saw several bodies scattered around the camp, young recruits and trainers who had refused to surrender their weapons and allow themselves to be tied up. The balance of the camp had been herded out at gunpoint and lay face down in the dirt, their hands tied behind them.

She paused when she saw Yursha lying on her stomach, and for one fearful second she thought Yursha too had been killed. She bent over her. Yursha raised her head and looked at Madison with those striking eyes.

Madison did not hesitate. She whispered, "I can take you with us. I have friends in the State Department who could arrange for you to stay in America."

Yursha nodded and Madison untied her hands and yelled to one of the commandos, "This one goes with us."

"No extra baggage," the commando responded. "Orders from the General."

Madison looked at him, her green eyes made wild by the killing around her. "This is not extra baggage, for chrissakes, this is CIA business. She goes. Tell your General I'll take responsibility."

She pulled the terrified Yursha to her feet and smiled reassuringly. "This wasn't really what you wanted after all, was it now?"

Two commandos came from building twelve, each holding one of Frank Rice's arms gently, and the whole group moved outside the fence to wait for the Black Hawk helicopters.

Steve Lakes counted the group as they ran

through the gate. "Move it, move it," he shouted. "We're on the clock here."

Seconds later the great fluttering birds sat down and picked up their cargo, including six Delta Force commandos who had lost their lives. As had an estimated forty others . . . The entire operation had taken only nine minutes.

CHAPTER SEVENTEEN

Mitchell Colby lifted his seventh floor telephone and was quiet for several seconds. Greg Abbott leaned forward impatiently, trying to read his expression. At length, Colby replaced the receiver and allowed himself a quick, satisfied grin. "White Flag is a complete success. Tahril has been neutralized. Madison and a three-year hostage should be arriving at Langley Air Force base in approximately eight hours."

Greg Abbott stood up and raised his fists

triumphantly. "Thank God, thank God. We did it," he said, barely able to maintain his composure.

Colby ran his finger down the classified file on his desk, then picked up his telephone. "Send someone to collect a file for the vault," he ordered, then smiled at Abbott. "The Providence file is officially closed."

* * * * *

Greg Allen Abbott and Marge Price had received approval from Mitchell Colby and had waited at the Air Force base to welcome Madison home and deliver her to CIA headquarters for debriefing. Abbott had wrapped his arms around her and greeted her as if she were a long lost friend, and Madison had returned his warm hugs with genuine affection.

Both Abbott and Marge Price had been greatly surprised to see Yursha following Madison off the plane. Madison explained the situation on the way to Langley and all parties involved had decided that it would be in Yursha's best interest to simply lie about her presence there. The government of the United States would never allow her to remain if they believed she had been training in the terrorist camp.

So it was decided that Yursha would be presented to the State Department as an informant who had helped Madison locate the terrorist camp and then found herself in a hostage situation.

"She has informed on radical Palestinian elements and worked closely with the West," Marge Price explained to Secretary of State James Jefferies. "To send her back would be murder. She wouldn't survive a day."

It took some stiff negotiations and all Marge Price's clout, but by the time Madison had endured a six-hour debriefing and a one-hour physical, Marge Price had secured a new identity for Yursha, who would now be permitted to live and work in the United States.

"What will I do?" Yursha asked, when the three of them sat in Marge's living room.

"What would you like to do?" Madison asked.

"Want schooling," Yursha answered without hesitation.

"Do you read and write English?" Marge inquired.

"Some. Not good."

Madison smiled. "We'll see about getting you into a college somewhere."

"American university free?"

"Don't worry about the money for now," Madison offered.

Yursha gave them a bright smile. "Americans rich. God bless U.S.A."

Madison looked at Marge Price who shrugged and laughed. "She heard that Lee Greenwood song on the radio. She's been singing it over and over. Wait until you hear the name she picked out for herself."

"June," Yursha announced. "June like the summer month. Last name McGuire. I saw what is Madison's name and Marge say McGuire, so I say McGuire will be my name too. June McGuire is new name."

Madison smiled. "I have the distinct feeling we're being hustled here."

"By the way," Marge began. "I've invited her to spend a few days here with me in D.C. until we find her an apartment. I know you have some business of your own to take care of in North Carolina. I'll show her around a little. It'll be fun. State owes me some time off."

"Thanks, Marge," Madison answered, looking at her watch. "I'm a bit anxious to get to that business, if you don't mind." She stood and looked at Yursha. "I'll see you in a few days Ms. June McGuire. And Marge, thanks so much for everything."

* * * * *

Madison grabbed a copy of the *Post* on her way out of D.C. and read the headlines with satisfaction.

FRANK RICE FREED

The article then went on to explain that in an effort to thaw relations with the U.S., radical factions in Beirut had released Frank Rice after months of pressure from the American government. The former hostage had been driven from Beirut to Damascus, the article read, where Syrian officials had then turned him over to the American authorities.

Madison shook her head. "Well, they got the headline right at least."

* * * * *

Terry Woodall pulled into the drive and parked. She rarely drove into the garage that Madison had

244

always used. It was too much like the bed she crawled into each night. She was never quite sure which side should be occupied or which side should be left empty.

Madison had liked that silly garage, she considered aimlessly as she unlocked the front door. She had used it faithfully and shut the automatic door behind her with the secretive appreciation of someone who had things to lock away. And Madison, Terry understood, had so much of herself she wanted to hide away in some little corner that was at least as deep as that garage.

She dropped her briefcase near the door and hung her shoulder bag over a chair arm as she went to the answering machine and checked for the blinking light. There were messages, as there usually were. One from the new secretary who delivered her message with an irritating snort that might have made Terry seriously consider discharging her, had she not feared repercussions from the Labor Board. Another two calls from clients who had recently taken to phoning her at home, as if they hadn't gotten their money's worth from her at the office already.

Deciding a glass of wine might calm the wave of tension that surged through her when she heard the needy voices on her machine, she went to the kitchen and opened the cabinet. For an instant she contemplated turning the bottle up right there, but finally reconsidered and reached for a glass.

And then she saw it. The envelope with Madison's name hastily scribbled across it, the envelope that had held her letter to Madison. It had been opened, slit along the top by a neat, precise stroke.

Terry barreled around the corner and took the stairs two at a time. She checked the bedroom, the study, the shower, the closets, and then ran back down the stairs and onto the deck.

Madison had reclaimed her spot on the beach where Terry had seen her sit so many times before with her green eyes fixed on the water, unseeing, lost in her own private thoughts.

Terry closed her eyes for a moment and then opened them quickly before the vision escaped her. *Oh God, she's come home. She needs me enough to forgive me for sending her away.*

Staring at Madison's back as Madison sat on their little strip of beach, Terry imagined them in their bed, imagined Madison rising from it quietly before Terry stirred, like a secret lover trying to beat the dawn.

How long will I have her this time? How long before they come for her because, in their wisdom, they're sure they need her more? How long before her bright eyes grow dull and her contentment once again fades?

As if sensing Terry's eyes on her, Madison turned and saw her standing there, and without hesitation she was on her feet running towards the house, running towards Terry, smiling, waving. And Terry knew then that Madison had never left her, never would truly leave her.

Author's Note

When I began writing this book it was my intention to not only, hopefully, create an entertaining and exciting book, but to also gain some understanding of terrorism in the Middle East today, especially terrorism as it relates to the Arab-Israeli conflict.

What I found was terrorism and violence on both sides, hatred on both sides, and finally a wish for peace and a hopefulness on both sides despite each side's conflicting and divergent views.

The Providence File focuses on a group of extremely *radical* Palestinian *terrorists*. I stress the words radical and terrorists here because although there are many radical and violent factions in operation, it is important to understand that all Palestinian groups are *not* considered radical and all Palestinians are not terrorists.

Today, there are many moderate groups hard at work with the goal of resolving the Arab-Israeli conflict through peaceful dialogue. I salute and support these groups, be they Palestinian or Israeli, Arab or Jew.

THE PROVIDENCE FILE by Amanda Kyle Williams. 256 pp.
Second espionage thriller featuring lesbian agent Madison McGuire
ISBN 0-941483-92-4 $8.95

I LEFT MY HEART by Jaye Maiman. 320 pp. A Robin Miller
Mystery. First in a series.   ISBN 0-941483-72-X   9.95

THE PRICE OF SALT by Patricia Highsmith (writing as Claire
Morgan). 288 pp. Classic lesbian novel, first issued in 1952 . . .
acknowledged by its author under her own, very famous, name.
ISBN 1-56280-003-5   8.95

SIDE BY SIDE by Isabel Miller. 256 pp. From beloved author of
Patience and Sarah.   ISBN 0-941483-77-0   8.95

SOUTHBOUND by Sheila Ortiz Taylor. 240 pp. Hilarious sequel
to *Faultline.*   ISBN 0-941483-78-9   8.95

STAYING POWER: LONG TERM LESBIAN COUPLES
by Susan E. Johnson. 352 pp. Joys of coupledom.
ISBN 0-941-483-75-4   12.95

SLICK by Camarin Grae. 304 pp. Exotic, erotic adventure.
ISBN 0-941483-74-6   9.95

NINTH LIFE by Lauren Wright Douglas. 256 pp. A Caitlin
Reece mystery. 2nd in a series.   ISBN 0-941483-50-9   8.95

PLAYERS by Robbi Sommers. 192 pp. Sizzling, erotic novel.
ISBN 0-941483-73-8   8.95

MURDER AT RED ROOK RANCH by Dorothy Tell. 224 pp.
First Poppy Dillworth adventure.   ISBN 0-941483-80-0   8.95

LESBIAN SURVIVAL MANUAL by Rhonda Dicksion.
112 pp. Cartoons!   ISBN 0-941483-71-1   8.95

A ROOM FULL OF WOMEN by Elisabeth Nonas. 256 pp.
Contemporary Lesbian lives.   ISBN 0-941483-69-X   8.95

MURDER IS RELATIVE by Karen Saum. 256 pp. The first
Brigid Donovan mystery.   ISBN 0-941483-70-3   8.95

PRIORITIES by Lynda Lyons 288 pp. Science fiction with
ISBN 0-941483-66-5   8.95

FOR DIVERSE INSTRUMENTS by Jane Rule. 208
ul romantic lesbian stories.   ISBN 0-941483-63-0   8.95

LESBIAN QUERIES by Hertz & Ertman. 112 pp. The questions
you were too embarrassed to ask.   ISBN 0-941483-67-3   8.95

CLUB 12 by Amanda Kyle Williams. 288 pp. Espionage thriller
featuring a lesbian agent!   ISBN 0-941483-64-9   8.95

DEATH DOWN UNDER by Claire McNab. 240 pp. 3rd Det.
Insp. Carol Ashton mystery.   ISBN 0-941483-39-8   8.95

MONTANA FEATHERS by Penny Hayes. 256 pp. Vivian and
Elizabeth find love in frontier Montana.   ISBN 0-941483-61-4   8.95

CHESAPEAKE PROJECT by Phyllis Horn. 304 pp. Jessie &
Meredith in perilous adventure.   ISBN 0-941483-58-4   8.95

LIFESTYLES by Jackie Calhoun. 224 pp. Contemporary Lesbian
lives and loves.   ISBN 0-941483-57-6   8.95

VIRAGO by Karen Marie Christa Minns. 208 pp. Darsen has
chosen Ginny.   ISBN 0-941483-56-8   8.95

WILDERNESS TREK by Dorothy Tell. 192 pp. Six women on
vacation learning "new" skills.   ISBN 0-941483-60-6   8.95

MURDER BY THE BOOK by Pat Welch. 256 pp. A Helen
Black Mystery. First in a series.   ISBN 0-941483-59-2   8.95

BERRIGAN by Vicki P. McConnell. 176 pp. Youthful Lesbian-
romantic, idealistic Berrigan.   ISBN 0-941483-55-X   8.95

LESBIANS IN GERMANY by Lillian Faderman & B. Eriksson.
128 pp. Fiction, poetry, essays.   ISBN 0-941483-62-2   8.95

THE BEVERLY MALIBU by Katherine V. Forrest. 288 pp. A
Kate Delafield Mystery. 3rd in a series.   ISBN 0-941483-47-9   16.95

THERE'S SOMETHING I'VE BEEN MEANING TO TELL
YOU Ed. by Loralee MacPike. 288 pp. Gay men and lesbians
coming out to their children.   ISBN 0-941483-44-4   9.95
                                       ISBN 0-941483-54-1   16.95

LIFTING BELLY by Gertrude Stein. Ed. by Rebecca Mark. 104
pp. Erotic poetry.   ISBN 0-941483-51-7   8.95
                          ISBN 0-941483-53-3   14.95

ROSE PENSKI by Roz Perry. 192 pp. Adult lovers in a long-term
relationship.   ISBN 0-941483-37-1   8.95

AFTER THE FIRE by Jane Rule. 256 pp. Warm, human novel
by this incomparable author.   ISBN 0-941483-45-2   8.95

SUE SLATE, PRIVATE EYE by Lee Lynch. 176 pp. The gay
folk of Peacock Alley are *all* cats.   ISBN 0-941483-52-5   8.95

CHRIS by Randy Salem. 224 pp. Golden oldie. Handsome Chris
and her adventures.   ISBN 0-941483-42-8   8.95

THREE WOMEN by March Hastings. 232 pp. Golden oldie. A
triangle among wealthy sophisticates.   ISBN 0-941483-43-6   8.95

RICE AND BEANS by Valeria Taylor. 232 pp. Love and
romance on poverty row.   ISBN 0-941483-41-X   8.95

PLEASURES by Robbi Sommers. 204 pp. Unprecedented
eroticism.   ISBN 0-941483-49-5   8.95

EDGEWISE by Camarin Grae. 372 pp. Spellbinding
adventure.   ISBN 0-941483-19-3   9.95

FATAL REUNION by Claire McNab. 216 pp. 2nd Det. Inspec.
Carol Ashton mystery.   ISBN 0-941483-40-1   8.95

KEEP TO ME STRANGER by Sarah Aldridge. 372 pp. Romance
set in a department store dynasty.   ISBN 0-941483-38-X   9.95

HEARTSCAPE by Sue Gambill. 204 pp. American lesbian in
Portugal.   ISBN 0-941483-33-9   8.95

IN THE BLOOD by Lauren Wright Douglas. 252 pp. Lesbian
science fiction adventure fantasy   ISBN 0-941483-22-3   8.95

THE BEE'S KISS by Shirley Verel. 216 pp. Delicate, delicious
romance.   ISBN 0-941483-36-3   8.95

RAGING MOTHER MOUNTAIN by Pat Emmerson. 264 pp.
Furosa Firechild's adventures in Wonderland. ISBN 0-941483-35-5   8.95

IN EVERY PORT by Karin Kallmaker. 228 pp. Jessica's sexy,
adventuresome travels.   ISBN 0-941483-37-7   8.95

OF LOVE AND GLORY by Evelyn Kennedy. 192 pp. Exciting
WWII romance.   ISBN 0-941483-32-0   8.95

CLICKING STONES by Nancy Tyler Glenn. 288 pp. Love
transcending time.   ISBN 0-941483-31-2   8.95

SURVIVING SISTERS by Gail Pass. 252 pp. Powerful love
story.   ISBN 0-941483-16-9   8.95

SOUTH OF THE LINE by Catherine Ennis. 216 pp. Civil War
adventure.   ISBN 0-941483-29-0   8.95

WOMAN PLUS WOMAN by Dolores Klaich. 300 pp. Supurb
Lesbian overview.   ISBN 0-941483-28-2   9.95

SLOW DANCING AT MISS POLLY'S by Sheila Ortiz Taylor.
96 pp. Lesbian Poetry   ISBN 0-941483-30-4   7.95

DOUBLE DAUGHTER by Vicki P. McConnell. 216 pp. A Nyla
Wade Mystery, third in the series.   ISBN 0-941483-26-6   8.95

These are just a few of the many Naiad Press titles — we are the oldest and
largest lesbian/feminist publishing company in the world. Please request a
complete catalog. We offer personal service; we encourage and welcome direct
mail orders from individuals who have limited access to bookstores carrying
our publications.